Blue Skies

DIANE WINTERS

ISBN 978-1-63525-252-1 (Paperback)
ISBN 978-1-63525-253-8 (Digital)

Christian Faith Publishing, Inc.
296 Chestnut Street
Meadville, PA 16335
www.christianfaithpublishing.com

Printed in the United States of America

I want to thank my husband for supporting my time in front of the computer and my daughter, Stacie, for helping me proofread.

Contents

Prologue

The halls were quiet. Ethereal. Page Lemon walked quietly down the halls, looking in doorways and an occasional closet. She stopped and looked around. "This has been a long time coming. I never thought I would see it completed." Her words echoed in the deserted building. "That's kind of creepy. But what do you expect when you wander around by yourself?" she thought. Page continued to walk the hallways, muted lighting showing her the way, air handlers humming, and the air conditioner regulating the entire facility from solar and wind power.

The new health care facility was state-of-the art and was designed by Page and her team. A large sum of the funds needed to make this happen came by way of fundraisers held by the Smith Falls Chamber of Commerce, and they were fortunate to find several entities that would loan them the remainder of what they needed. In addition, there were a number of large donations that would be used as naming rights for various wings and equipment. The community had been without their hospital long enough and Page was glad to see the construction finally coming to an end. The doors would open as early as the following week and the staff planned to train and orient starting bright and early in the morning. George Cranshaw, the CEO, was just as anxious to get going as the community and staff. Everyone was excited to have a grand opening and start taking care of patients once again. In the interim, the community had to make a forty minute drive to the next town for their healthcare issues. Less than two years ago, the neighboring communities had been spared the tornado by only two miles to the east and a mile on the north. The bouncing tornado finally lifted and dissipated just before reaching those areas.

As she stood in front of the large glass windows in the anteroom, she watched a car turn and drive up the long driveway. "I hope they don't think we are open!" The car slowed and then stopped outside the doors. Page watched quietly as the driver sat there for a time before opening the door to get out. When Page realized who it was, she stared at the imposing figure. "What the heck?"

Chapter 1

Page graduated from high school and left home directly for college that summer. She wanted to get away from home; and between working, saving, and earning several college scholarships, she was able to escape. She got herself set up at a college two hundred miles away and never looked back. Home wasn't a good memory. Actually, Page felt that she really had no home growing up, merely a roof over her head. Page vowed to make it on her own and never wanted to have to look or come back to her roots. That was twenty-six years ago.

The self-made businesswoman had come into her own early in life and continued to make a name for herself. Broken relationships were scattered along the way, and most men were threatened by her controlling and divisive behavior. The only good thing to come out of a past (and last) relationship was her daughter, Chase. The father had left to take a job on the coast several years ago after learning Page was pregnant. Doug Reilly's reaction was all too similar to how her father reacted to having a daughter. Doug wanted Page to have an abortion. Having a child was not in his plans for the future. Page said good riddance and threw herself into making a happy life for Chase. She never contacted Doug once Chase was born. She never felt bad about it as Doug had never contacted her either.

Chase was now sixteen and thriving in school. She was involved in every sport and activity available and had truckloads of friends—something Page never had growing up. Although Chase was well-rounded and happy, Page was often depressed when thinking about her own life growing up. She was ecstatic about how well Chase was turning out, and she was thrilled she could help make that happen. Life was truly good for them both.

Then, the tornado struck. Literally. Page woke up to news that a tornado tore through her hometown and took out several buildings and homes. As she watched the news coverage, she realized it not only destroyed several businesses—including the hospital—it also took her old neighborhood. Death and destruction were everywhere. Page sat in shock as the coverage showed an aerial view of what was once her hometown. The destruction looked like a box of matchsticks was dumped out all over town. The tornado was classified as an E5 and covered a strip a mile and a half wide. It was on the ground for over twenty-five miles before bouncing up and down for another thirty miles. Her hometown of Smith Falls was devastated.

When Chase came home from school, she found her mom still sitting in front of the news.

"Mom! Are you still watching that? Why?" Page looked at Chase and sighed. Page never told Chase she had grown up in Smith Falls. Page had lived in Johnstown for so long she considered it home and never had any reason to let Chase think otherwise. Her parents were an unknown variable in this current crisis. Page had no idea whether or not they were even alive before the storm hit, let alone after her old home was destroyed. The guilt inside surprised her. She looked up at Chase again. In a heartbeat, she realized hiding her past did nothing to heal the pain. Considering the anger, guilt, and pain she felt watching the news, she knew it was time to let the past go. And more than that, Page realized that she had been selfish to not tell

Chase about her grandparents. Page was hit with the realization that she needed to clear up the past or she could never go forward.

"Sit down, Chase. Let me tell you a story that is long overdue." Chase sat across from her mom. "What is it, Mom? What is going on?" Page muted the television and sighed again. She looked at Chase and tried to decide where to start and how much this could affect them both. Page decided she needed to start at the very beginning—as a child.

"You are old enough to know the truth about how I grew up, and I am way overdue in admitting it to not only you, but also to myself. I have denied talking about my past to protect myself from the memories just so I didn't have to deal with them." She struggled to continue. "My past came tumbling down today and confronted me big time, and now, I need to face that past and share it with you. Chase, I'm going to need your support and understanding for what I'm about to tell you. You may very well be upset with me by the time I'm done, but at this point, I'm pretty ashamed of myself for not facing my past with you. Shoot. I didn't even want to admit I had a past! This will be very difficult for me, and I would appreciate you holding questions until I get to the end. OK?" Chase nodded in agreement and gave her mom a big hug. "It will be fine, Mom. We can do this together."

Page took a big breath and began telling her story, beginning with the fact that she had been raised in Smith Falls by a couple that should not have been parents. Her mother drank to excess and her father, although a good provider, hated having a daughter around. Page practically raised herself. Her neighbor, Grace Pinkal, was like a grandmother to her, and Page spent more time at Grace's house than her own

Grace had been alone for years and never had children. She was a portly woman, wore her gray hair in a bun every day. When she worked in the kitchen, her favorite room in the house, she always donned a smile and a faded apron covered in daffodils. Page never felt like she had parents. She was too skinny and clumsy, very introverted. Her dark wavy hair seemed to never be under control. The relationship was mutually beneficial. Grace had watched Page come home from school and then stay outside by herself many times. She noticed that her parents never took her anywhere and Page seemed to flounder. One hot summer day, Grace approached Page with her grin and a handful of freshly baked cookies. They soon became great friends. Grace had no idea how her mother ever kept Page in clothes and shoes. At times, Grace would pick something up from the thrift store for her; so she would have a warm sweater or a nice dress. Page began to do her homework at Grace's kitchen table and had after-school snacks. Sometimes, they even had supper together when Page's mom was too inebriated to cook, which seemed to be more often as time passed. Her father would scream and yell and carry on when he came home to find her mother passed out. Page always knew when to be gone after she came home from school and find her mother on the couch. She would then head over to Grace's house until bedtime. Her father rotated between not noticing her absence and not caring where she was.

Not only did Grace help with her homework and provide her a steady mentor, but Page also learned the Bible. Grace read her passages before she would go home every night and took her to church on Sunday. Eventually, Page came to understand the need for Jesus in her life; and she became saved and baptized. Grace was so proud and stood with Page as she was baptized. Grace helped Page to realize that her parents would never be able to care for her as long as they only thought of themselves. Grace and Page prayed for them every day they were together.

As Page grew into a teenager, Grace became ill. Grace had hired someone to come in and help her for a few hours during the day, and then, Page would care for her in the evening. At times, Page stayed overnight when Grace was becoming frailer. When it became too unsafe at home, Grace made the decision to go to the nursing home for care. Page would visit several times a week and spend most of the day on Sunday with her. They attended church in the chapel; and now, Page was the one reading the Bible passages to Grace. Grace was the one adult that Page could depend on and was always there for her. Page knew that when Grace died and went to meet Jesus, she would always be grateful to Grace for being in her life and bringing her the Word of God. Grace showed her love of parenting and love of God. Grace showed her the meaning of grace.

By the time Grace died, Page was developing into a beautiful young lady and was able to socialize at school and church. She still had few good friends, but no one was ever invited to her house. Occasionally, she would have someone stop by Grace's home to study for tests, but there was no way she would take them to her own home next door. She would refer to Grace as Grandma to keep others from questioning their relationship.

A couple of weeks after Grace died, a lawyer was on Page's doorstep. Ms. Yancy told her that Grace had left everything to Page and that the house would be sold. The money would be placed in a trust for her until she was twenty-five. Ms. Yancy gave her a business card and told her she could come by and see her anytime she needed funds. She was also given the keys to Grace's old car. The licensure and insurance was to be paid for until Page graduated from college. Page would need to get a part-time job to pay for the gas and to save up for college. Grace didn't have enough to pay for her college tuition because of the nursing home expenses, but Ms. Yancy said that Grace knew that Page was smart enough to win scholarships.

Ms. Yancy said she would help with any paperwork that needed completed and had already gone to court to be considered her personal guardian. Grace had written and tracked the time Page spent with her for several years, and Ms. Yancy had used that information in court. The judge found no reason to deny Ms. Yancy guardianship although he wanted to remove Page from her home and place her in foster care. Ms. Yancy assured the judge that Page was not in danger and that she would personally see to her needs. Page no longer had to attempt to discuss her future plans or needs with her parents. The Lemons were issued a certified copy of the guardianship papers, but it had lain on the table unopened for months.

Chase continued to sit in awe. Although Chase rarely asked about it, her mother had always brushed her past off as no big deal. Chase offered to get some soft drinks when her mom paused. She had no questions with the story so far, but she could see why her mom didn't want to talk about her past. Page reorganized her thoughts after taking a drink and continued her story.

Page continued to work hard at her studies and was an honor student. She worked part-time at the local grocery store. Her parents never asked her where she was or what she was doing. When the time came for graduation, Page notified her parents, left an announcement on the refrigerator, and sent one to Ms. Yancy. She graduated with honors and, as the salutatorian, gave a speech that Ms. Yancy assisted Page in writing. During the ceremony, Ms. Yancy was seated in the spot her parents should have been. Page missed Grace at this important time of her life. She left a flower on the chair next to Ms. Yancy in memory of Grace and honored her in her speech. Page knew her parents wouldn't attend, and tried not to let it hurt when eyeing the audience and all the other parents and family members that attended.

After graduation was over, Page went home and packed her meager personal belongings. It all fit in the back seat of her car. In her room, she left a Bible for her mother with passages bookmarked and underlined. She left a note to both parents, telling them good-bye. She told them she would continue to pray for her mother to get sober and her father to stop hating her. She signed it with her love for them and that she was now off to college and ready to start her own life. She said a casual good-bye to her parents on the way out the door. They didn't question why she was loading the car, just as they never questioned where she got the car in the first place. It always amazed her that her parents had no idea if she was in the house or not and that she had a job, and she didn't even know if they had any idea she had just graduated from high school and would never be back.

Page sighed as she drove away. She took one last look in the mirror at her old home and drove to her new home in Johnstown, an apartment that Ms. Yancy had helped her find. It was a furnished apartment in a quiet neighborhood. The landlady reminded Page of Grace in her younger years and felt comfortable the minute they met. Looking back, Ms. Yancy probably knew that when she helped her find an apartment. Page had a lot to be thankful for in Ms. Yancy. The only thing that Page requested was to not hear any news from her hometown. She was starting over fresh and didn't want any distraction. Summer school started two weeks after Page moved to Johnstown. In the meantime, she found a part-time job in her neighborhood at a local grocery store. There was the perfect church for her two blocks down from her apartment.

Life was just beginning for Page, and she was both scared and excited. She kept in touch frequently with Ms. Yancy for the next six years as she graduated with her master's degree in architecture. Going to school and carrying a full load—even through the summertime— allowed for an early graduation for Page. Ms. Yancy was there for her proud moment. Page graduated with honors once again and had several job offers. Ms. Yancy helped go over Page's personal goals and eliminate jobs that had no bearing on her future.

Page had grown to love architecture while still in high school. She was flipping through magazines in the library and kept going back through several articles on architectural studies. When Page had visited Grace in the nursing home, she felt that there were several areas that could be improved upon to be more efficient and would discuss those with Grace. If Grace was in the hospital, they would discuss the hospital features. Grace encouraged Page to extend her imagination to the not-so-obvious needs of staff and patients alike.

Page worked with the high school counselor to arrange her studies to fit her graduating needs and found a college that suited her. Ms. Yancy helped her with the college application; and between the counselor and Ms. Yancy, she applied for several scholarships in her chosen field. With Page earning the salutatorian position in her class, she was given a free-ride scholarship to the college of her choice and enough scholarships that she would require only enough funds for rent, food, and necessities. Page and Ms. Yancy decided the money from Grace could be used for a different car or other emergencies and would always be there if she decided to not work while in school.

Page opted to work for a small architectural firm that had worked in the healthcare field and was looking for someone to expand that area of expertise. The money offered wasn't as high as other job offers, but the company itself felt right to Page. The small firm was now a multi-million dollar entity and Page was now a partner—Gregg, Fielding, and Lemon. Page played a large part as to why the firm had been so successful in the healthcare field. She was unrelenting, and her imagination kept their drawings fresh and new. Her niche in the field was specialized, but wildly impressive. The firm was sought after by companies in several surrounding states to provide the ideas and follow-through for updating and new facilities.

After Chase was born, Page stopped the majority of her traveling. She found a modest condo to purchase and made a permanent home for them. Page occasionally would take Chase on trips during school and summer breaks, and they would see the sites. Page didn't want to be an absentee parent and limited her time away. Since she was handling parenting by herself, she was very adamant about it. Her partners were both family men and appreciated her skills enough to allow her the ability to be both a mom and a partner. The firm would send other staff, and Page would Skype with the facilities as needed.

Page was independently wealthy now; and even though Ms. Yancy had retired several years previous, they continued to stay in touch. Ms. Yancy would still give her advice as needed. The original trust fund had seldom been touched, and Ms. Yancy eventually helped her place it in Chase's name. Page would add funds every year, and it had grown into a huge portfolio. Her daughter would never have to fear for the future or give up her personal life and work day and night like she did. Page still lived in her original condo; and even though she could afford bigger and better one, this was her home that she made for Chase. She didn't want unnecessary changes in their life, and Page loved the permanence of it.

Page got up and shut the television off. "Let's have supper, then we can discuss more later on. It will give you a chance to think about everything." Chase agreed, and they went to the kitchen together arm in arm.

Chapter 2

Doug Reilly grew up in a rough neighborhood outside of Johnstown. He and the local boys ran around day and night and frequently got into trouble harassing girls, dogs, and even the elderly. Store owners knew they were shoplifting but couldn't catch them. He was a spindly boy from lack of food and too much exercise running the streets. His blond hair was frequently unkempt, and his blue eyes shown bright with energy. Doug didn't see anything wrong in his unlawful behavior. He knew his mother worked two jobs to keep some food on the table and the rent paid. His mother had no idea what trouble he was in most of the time. Even if she knew, Doug thought she didn't have time to care. She would come home exhausted, would go to bed, and would be gone before he got up in the morning. His mom did care if he went to school, but learning wasn't on his agenda. Doug frequently skipped classes he hated and only pretended to like others he attended. The teachers frequently ignored his antics.

Doug was twelve when Mr. Cheetum, the math teacher, held him back after class. Doug was barraged with questions he didn't much feel like answering—Why didn't he do his homework? Was it too hard? Did he need a tutor? Doug simply sat there and stared at the floor. Even though Doug liked him, he didn't want the teacher to know. After all, Doug was Mr. Tough Guy. If Doug were skipping classes, he never skipped Mr. Cheetum's.

Then, Mr. Cheetum did something Doug didn't expect. He put an arm around his shoulders and told Doug he was sorry. He offered to help Doug with his work every day. Then, he asked him something even more unexpected. Mr. Cheetum asked Doug to come home with him that evening for supper and meet his wife. Doug stared at Mr. Cheetum. "What do you mean come home with you for supper? Are you crazy? Why would you want a troublemaker like me around your house?" Mr. Cheetum laid his hand on Doug's arm and stated, "You look like you could use a real friend and a good meal. Come on. School's out. Let's go see what my wife is making for supper, and we can shoot a few hoops while we wait." Doug had no idea what else to do, so he followed Mr. Cheetum out the door and got into his car.

Mr. Cheetum became an integral part of Doug's life thereafter. He taught him purpose, kept him off the streets; and both Mr. and Mrs. Cheetum began teaching him the Bible. Even though Doug only had Mr. Cheetum for one year at school, the Cheetums became an integral part of Doug's life. Doug invited them to meet his mother, and they both began to attend the church the Cheetums attended. Eventually, both Doug and his mother became baptized Christians. Doug continued to use Mr. Cheetum as a tutor throughout school and felt that without him coming into his life when he did, he would probably be sitting behind bars as a few of his old neighbor buddies found themselves. His mother often thanked the Cheetums for being there for Doug when she hadn't been. His father had left shortly after Doug was born and left her with little money and a lot of debt. Her love of Doug fell to the side as she attempted to provide a roof over their head and food in the cupboard. She hadn't realized how much trouble Doug was getting into and was thankful for Cheetums showing them both a better future.

Doug went on to college in Johnstown. He was able to live at home to save money but took a part-time job to take care of what student loans couldn't cover. Because of Mr. Cheetum's influence, Doug had taken an interest in accounting. After graduation, he found an entry-level position at a large firm in Johnstown. His plan to make something of himself became all consuming. Nothing was going to stop him from becoming wealthy. He wanted to buy a nice house for his mother, so she could retire and be comfortable. He worked hard and continued to impress his employers with his work ethic and ability to manage his accounts.

By the time he was twenty-eight, Doug had advanced in his career enough that he was supervising junior accountants. He started to cut back on his long hours and began to go out and enjoy himself more. He ran into a woman named Page Lemon during social hour at a club one evening, and they hit it off immediately. Both were driven and knew what they wanted out of life. They agreed to see each other in a couple of weeks but instead met up two days later and began a close relationship. Doug had grown into a handsome blond-haired gentleman, and his bright blue eyes now shown bright with energy. He had never considered himself good looking and had never realized the effect he had on women. Page, who herself had turned into a very pretty dark-haired woman, was immediately attracted to Doug's zest for life; and his eyes seemed to draw her in every time she looked at him.

As their relationship continued to grow, their friends would include them both as a couple when inviting them over for cookouts and other activities. Everyone, including Page and Doug, felt that their future together was secure; and they would eventually be married. A few months later, Doug was offered a job on the coast to head up a new branch office. The money was fantastic, and the benefits were too good to be true. He had finally made partner and was given his own office. He met up with Page at her apartment to tell her the good news. In his excitement, Doug talked on and on about the new opportunity and how he had made the "big time." As he started to wind down, he realized Page was quiet.

"Why are you so quiet? Aren't you excited for me?" Page stared at him and replied, "Where am I in this new life of yours? Where do I fit in?" Doug stopped for a moment. He hadn't even considered Page in his new quest. Doug scratched his head and looked a little sheepish. "I'm sorry. I guess I just assumed you would be happy for me and would come with me." Page looked at him like he had grown two heads. "You thought I would give up my partnership to go to the coast with you? Just like that?" Doug sighed. "I'm sorry. I hadn't really given that any thought. This is my dream. I guess I thought you would come with me, we'd get married, and you could find something out there. I don't know. I was just so wrapped up in the offer I didn't give you any thought. You already made partner, so you know how much this means to me." Doug was beginning to get frustrated. He wanted this job and partnership. After all the hard work he put in, he felt he deserved it; and there was no way Page was going to take this from him. Page's mind started to freeze. She knew that this was what Doug had been working for. She knew it had almost consumed him over time, but there was no way she was giving up her own job to move with him. He hadn't even considered her during the whole process or talked to her about it before accepting the job. Page felt the tension in the room continue to grow. "I'm pregnant."

"*What?*" Doug looked at her and balled up his fists. "Are you kidding me?" He continued to rant and rave about how she had set him up, that Page was trying to keep him tied down and not be able to become partner. Doug paced wildly back and forth across the living room. He even demanded that she have an abortion because Doug wasn't going to take care of this baby trap. The whole time Doug was yelling about not having their child, all Page could think about was her own father not wanting a child and being ignored for eighteen years. Page got up and calmly asked Doug to leave, that she didn't want to hear from him again, and to not ever worry about a baby trap in the future. She stood, quietly holding the door open. Doug paused and looked at her a final time, then stormed out the door. He stopped and yelled at her again to have an abortion and to never call him again as he jumped in his car to leave. Page stared at the only man she had ever loved as he drove away. She closed the door, dropped to the floor, and sobbed uncontrollably for the next hour.

Doug took his job on the coast without hesitation. Instead of buying his mother a house, he made sure she was moved into a nice assisted living facility at his expense. She was deteriorating, and Doug wanted to make sure she was safe. Doug's job required him to work long hours and socialize often with clients and would-be clients. He made more money than he knew what to do with. He dated a few women, but no one struck a chord with him. Women flirted with him all the time because of his status, but he showed no long-term interest in shallow relationships.

After a few years, Doug helped open another office in the south. He flew back and forth, continuing to increase his net worth; but his life only felt emptier. His mother had died of a massive heart attack a year ago, and he had no other family to visit. When he flew back to Johnstown for the funeral and to tidy up the estate, he thought about finding Page. He talked himself out of it, but he occasionally wondered if Page had the baby or an abortion. Doug never heard from her again, so he assumed she had aborted the child. After all, they had both been job-oriented people. Doug did stop to see Mr. and Mrs. Cheetum to catch up and even went to church with them. A feeling of warmth surrounded him during church, and it stayed with him for the rest of his visit.

When Doug got back to the coast, he realized what he was missing. He had strayed from the church all these years. The only time he had gone to church was with the Cheetums and his mother. Doug's guilt only intensified when he realized he had no idea where he could go to church at home. He dug out the phone book and started leafing through the listings. One was an easy drive from his apartment. He tapped his pencil on the pad in front of him. Yes, it was way overdue.

On Sunday, Doug pulled himself together and headed to church. He found the pastor friendly, and many of the congregation stopped to introduce themselves. Doug enjoyed the service, music, and the people. The warmth returned to his soul. He vowed to come every Sunday he was in town. Doug set up an appointment with the pastor to visit later in the week. He couldn't continue on the way he was living his life and needed some spiritual guidance. Thanks to the Cheetums, Doug knew what he really needed in his life and what he had been missing all these years. He had strayed early on in his career, but it was over due to come back to the truth.

* * * * * * * * *

"OK. Where were we?" Page said as they sat back in the living room and got comfortable. Chase nodded. "Let's see. I know about you growing up, college, and your current job. I think you left out something. Or someone." Page cringed inwardly. She hadn't told Chase much about Doug. There really wasn't too much to tell her, considering she hadn't heard from him in almost seventeen years. She did owe Chase a better explanation. As long as she was spilling her guts, it was best she include the father of her only child. Chase looked at her mother expectantly. She often looked in the mirror and wondered if she looked anything like her father. Chase knew it was a touchy subject, and she heard enough from her friends about parental problems and relationships. Chase had been lucky to have a great relationship with her mother.

"This could be a long night, but you deserve some answers. I expected you to bring your father up long before now, but let's get this all on the table tonight." Page went on to explain the tenuous relationship that occurred at the time of their breakup. She explained that considering her own father's behavior, there was no way she would allow that around her own child. It was easier to let Doug leave and tend to business on her own; and evidently, Doug wanted it that way too. She reassured Chase that Ms. Yancy had information on how to get a hold of Doug in case something happened to Page while she was growing up. Page had no idea if he was still with the same company or not. "I loved him with all my heart, but when he was so livid about me being pregnant, I loved you more. I haven't met anyone in the last sixteen years that made me want to start a relationship. That is part of the reason I am so protective of you and want you to enjoy life and see what is out there, just waiting for you. I just hope you have better luck than me!" Chase giggled. The sound served as a welcome, albeit brief, reminder that the pain she felt while telling Chase these stories could not touch her daughter.

"Do you think he got married and started his own family now?' said Chase. Page replied, "I have no idea. It's been a long time. Anything could have happened. I will let you think on this for a while; and then, if you want to meet him, you can see if you can reach him and ask if he would meet you. I don't believe he knows you exist, so it could be a shock and one that he may not appreciate at all. You would need to be prepared to be denied. And if he hasn't changed, then you are better off not meeting him." Chase gave that some thought and said she would definitely have to get input from her friends or her pastor. The one thing that Page had done after Doug left was to return to church. She had drifted away when she began working so many hours. She went back to the church she had gone to while in college, and Chase was brought up in the loving surroundings of the congregation.

Page got up and dug in a desk drawer file. "I think you are old enough to see this." Page handed the trust portfolio to her daughter. She explained, "This was the trust fund that Grace had set up for me when I was a teen. I didn't need much of it, so Ms. Yancy has put it in your name. As you can see, I have added to it over time; and you are one rich little lady now. You will never want for anything your whole life. I just wanted to make sure you were taken care of if something happened to me, and you didn't have a father to care for you."

Chase was shocked. She had no idea her Mother had so much money. She knew that they always had what they needed and that her Mother provided well for her. It was well known that she donated a good portion to church activities and helped send a group to Haiti yearly. Since she was old enough now, Chase had been able to go the last couple of years. Chase reached over and grabbed her mother and held on tight. She thanked her for caring so much and reassured her mother that she would follow closely in her footsteps and be generous in the right things and not waste money on frivolous items. Chase handed the portfolio back to her mother with shaking hands, then grabbed her again in a big hug.

"You have made me proud, little girl. You are turning into a beautiful lady, and you already have a generous heart. Now! Before we continue on the mush train, let's see where this story needs to go next! The one thing I don't know is if your grandparents are alive. They could have died years ago or in the tornado. I have ignored my hometown for years. I don't have any idea who lives there, and that includes my parents. I guess it's time to call up Ms. Yancy and ask. *Oh!* I hope her home hasn't been hit too! I need to call her first thing in the morning. And communication might be sketchy too. Oh my! I hadn't even thought about her! Now, I really feel guilty!" Chase laughed at her mother. "It's OK, Mom. You've had a lot on your mind today, and it's only eight. Let's give it a try now, and then we'll know."

Page found her phone and called Ms. Yancy. The phone rang several times; and just as Page was going to hang up, Ms. Yancy answered. "Page! I'm so glad you called! I've been so busy here. Our apartments were spared on my side of the street. But across the street, it took the roofs off. We are taking in as many people as we can in each apartment to help out." Page hadn't said a word yet, but she could hear commotion in the background. "Ms. Yancy, we are so glad you are OK. That is so brave of you to take in strangers. Do you have time to talk?" "Of course, my dear. And I believe I know what you are going to ask me. You want to know about your parents."

"Ms. Yancy, you always could read my mind. I need to know if they are alive or not."

"Listen missy, I've waited a lot of years to talk to you about them. So if you want to know, you are going to come here and see me."

"What? You aren't going to tell me?"

"*No!* And I have my hands full right now. I could use your help. So are you coming or not?" Page looked at Chase. Chase shrugged at the look. She had no idea what was being said. Page replied, "We'll drive out on the weekend. I can't have Chase missing school. Is that OK?"

"That will be fine, but make a reservation somewhere before you come. Or you won't have a place to stay. Everything is full here and in the surrounding areas with this mess on our hands."

"I will make some calls. We will see you soon." Page stared at Chase. Chase looked back in curiosity. *"What?"*

"We have to go and see her or she won't answer any questions. Isn't she a hoot?" Chase and Page both laughed. It helped release some of the day-long tension.

Page hugged Chase. "I think we've covered enough ground for now. The decision has been made for me. We are going to drive to Smith Falls and look for my past in the future."

Chapter 3

The closest motel Page could find was a bed and breakfast forty minutes away from Smith Falls in the small town of Louden. It was located on the edge of town, and she found it easily. Chase enjoyed looking through all the rooms in the house due to the vast collection of knickknacks from every era imaginable. They had to share a bed, but it was large. And the mattress was comfortable. As they threw themselves into settling in for the evening, Chase found several books to choose from and some board games. "Mom, do you want to play any of these?" Page looked at each of them, and they chose one they both knew but hadn't played in some time. They spent an enjoyable evening lounging and laughing.

Before turning in for the night, Chase suggested they pray for what they would find the next day and for Page to be able to handle the knowledge. "Chase, you are always so intuitive. You are such a blessing to me." They held hands and prayed together for the trip they were making and for Page to make the right decisions. They also prayed for the town of Smith Falls and for God to provide hope and courage to the residents of that town. Page and Chase turned in early in hopes of getting several hours of sleep before their trek into Smith Falls.

Saturday morning brought bright sunshine through the lacy window coverings and awakened Chase. Page was already up and had showered. Chase groaned and followed suit. Breakfast was waiting downstairs for them, and they needed to hit the road as Ms. Yancy would be waiting for them.

As they drove into Smith Falls, there was devastation everywhere. Emergency vehicles lined the streets, television and radio reporters were everywhere, and residents were walking around with dazed looks on their faces. Page drove around the outskirts of town, attempting to miss the traffic and destruction. Finding Ms. Yancy's apartments took almost an hour due to the detours Page had to take. Once in the complex area, they had to park and walk a few blocks to get to her group of apartments. Page and Chase remained speechless as they kept looking at all the devastation. They stood on the sidewalk outside of Ms. Yancy's apartments and looked across the street to the matchsticks that once were apartment buildings. Another group had lost the roofing, and some of the siding was hanging off. "How did anyone survive through that?" said Page. Chase just shook her head. "Come on, Mom. Let's find Ms. Yancy and see what they need us to get for them." Page smiled at Chase. Chase always thought of others first.

They walked up to Ms. Yancy's apartment and knocked on the door. Ms. Yancy opened the door and held them both in a big hug; tears filled her eyes. Page looked over her shoulder and saw an additional six strangers in the living room. "So I see you have new roommates," said Page. Ms. Yancy brought them in and introduced them to everyone. "Let's go out on the back patio. Believe it or not, the furniture is still there." They all went through the sliding door and found a seat. "Ms. Yancy, this is terrible. What I saw on TV is nothing like in person. I can't believe how hard it was for me to get here. And some of the landmarks are gone."

"I know, dear, but thank God we only lost two people. There were several injuries, of course, but we had enough notice with the sirens to get everyone from our apartments to the shelters."

Looking from the patio side of the building, nothing looked out of place. There was even an occasional bird chirping, the flowers were blooming, and the trees still had most of their leaves. The three of them sat for a while involved in their own thoughts. Ms. Yancy broke the spell. "Your parents are gone, Page, and have been for a couple of years." Page looked at Ms. Yancy and sighed, several thoughts going through her—guilt, relief, guilt, despair, guilt. Always the guilt. "They actually had an accident. Someone hit them head on in the middle of a terrible rainstorm. I was told they died instantly. I know you told me not to tell you anything about them, but I wanted to call you several times. Page had tears in her eyes. "I'm so sorry Ms. Yancy. They just cared so little about me my whole life I just didn't want to know about them. I think now it was my own type of retribution in case they ever wondered what happened to me."

Chase sat quietly, watching her Mom process the latest news. She could see her work through her feelings. She reached out and held her hand and remained quiet. Ms. Yancy looked back at Page. "I also need to tell you that your Mother finally quit drinking but not until about a year before she died. She had your letter and Bible with her at the time of her death. They were coming home from an AA meeting. I'm told that both your parents realized too late what they had done to you and had only realized in the last few months before they died what they missed out on. I handled the estate and found your graduation announcement still hanging on the refrigerator. I have the Bible, letters, and a few other mementos I thought you would want to keep. Everything else was sold and the money invested in Chase's portfolio." Page began to cry softly. Chase held her in a soft embrace and rubbed her back. "All those years. I prayed all those years for them. Do you think they found Jesus before they died?" Ms. Yancy closed her eyes, silent tears flowing. "I would like to believe that. They began going to our church and were being counseled. Our pastor could probably tell you. I had them do a graveside service only. I requested that the caskets be closed as the accident wasn't kind to them." Page looked over at Ms. Yancy and reached for her. "Thank you so much for everything you have done for our family. I'm sorry I was so hard headed that I didn't allow you to talk about my parents sooner."

"It's OK, Page. Life is hard sometimes. Just look around Smith Falls." Page looked around. "It's just so final. Did they ever ask about me?" "They just asked me to continue to care for you. It's like they knew they had blown it and didn't feel like they could ask anything of you once they sorted through things and began to realize you grew up without them." Page looked at Chase and thought of Doug missing out on so much of Chase's life. Even though Page attempted to be a great mother, she realized how much a father could have meant to Chase all those formative years.

Ms. Yancy went back inside to see if anyone needed anything and left Page and Chase to think about the information and get emotions under control. "What do you think, Chase? Is Mom an idiot for not keeping track of her own parents?" Page sniffled and found a Kleenex to tidy up her swollen eyes and runny nose. "Mom, the last few days have been really weird. I have found out you are from Smith Falls, who my dad is, I had grandparents until a couple of years ago, and I came to a town that looks like it's been blown up into kindling. Talk about an emotional trip!" "Oh, Chase! I'm so sorry! What a mess I've made of everything! I've denied you a father, grandparents, Smith Falls, and your heritage. I'm so selfish!" Page began to cry in earnest, and Chase joined her. The emotions were running strong between the two of them. "It's OK, Mom, truly. You had it a lot tougher growing up than I have. It will be all right."

Ms. Yancy came back out to the patio and watched the two crying and blowing their noses. "OK, girls. Time to put on your big girl panties and a smile on your faces!" Page and Chase looked up at Ms. Yancy, then at each other; and they all three cracked up laughing. All three hugged each other again, blew their noses, and put smiles on their faces. Chase looked at Ms. Yancy and stated, "Now that the hard part is over, what do you need us to do?" They all smiled at each other, and Ms. Yancy pulled them inside to help fix lunch.

After the lunch mess was cleaned up, Page and Chase made a list of things they needed to bring back to the apartment complex the following day. Page made an additional list of things she could do for the community. She gave the list to Chase to add to as they drove around town and talked to community leaders. Page would be able to provide a variety of items once she got back to Johnstown. She had already talked to her church and other groups about gathering items for Smith Falls and sending a truck with supplies that follow-ing week. Time was of the essence for many people. While making her list, she made sure she coordinated with the Red Cross and other area groups to provide items of need without duplicating services. Everyone would play an important part in the effort to provide relief, and Page didn't want to get in anyone's way.

The last stop Page made was to find the CEO of the hospital. The building was all but completely destroyed. The clinic had been attached to the hospital, and there was a big pile of rubble in its spot. Three walls of the hospital were caved in, and the safe room that the patients and staff were in was the only room not damaged. Although the community of thirty thousand was small, losing their hospital and clinic would be devastating. The triage for the injured was being handled in the high school gym. The local pharmacies brought in as many emergency supplies they could carry and had their own staff run back and forth as prescriptions needed to be filled. Generators were brought in from the farming community and from the hardware store and set up to provide electricity for the gym, pharmacies, and the one grocery store not affected.

Page asked where she could locate Mr. Cranshaw and was told he would be at the gym. When she walked in and asked where she might locate him, he was sitting alone in the bleachers, staring off into space. Page and Chase walked up to where he was. "Mr. Cranshaw?" He looked at Page blankly then refocused. "I'm sorry. Do I know you?" he said. "No sir, my name is Page Lemon. And this is my daughter, Chase." "Nice to meet you, ladies. What can I do for you?"

"Sir, I want to give something back to this community as I was raised here. I'm an architect and would like our firm to help rebuild the community healthcare facility. I know it's pretty early in the game to be talking about rebuilding, but the hospital and clinic need to be replaced as quickly as possible." Mr. Cranshaw looked at both Page and Chase and started to cry. And then, he began to wail. Everyone in the gym stopped what they were doing and stared. Page and Chase looked at each other and were both embarrassed. "I see we've come at a bad time, sir. We will just be going. I'll leave my information with someone here." Page and Chase turned to leave and followed their path back down out of the bleachers and toward the doctors working with patients on the floor of the gym. Mr. Cranshaw continued to cry loudly as they walked away. "I apologize. I don't know what I said to upset him so." One of the doctors shook his head. "It's OK. He lost his wife in the tornado. She was home at the time, and the house took a direct hit." Page looked appalled. "I'm so sorry! I had no idea! I feel like such a fool now blathering on and on about helping rebuild the hospital." Page pulled out a business card and gave it to the doctor. "I specialize in the healthcare field. Please hang on to my card. I grew up here and want to help give back when the community feels they are ready." The doctor agreed to hang on to it and talk to Mr. Cranshaw at a later time. Page thanked him, and they left.

"Wow, Mom! That was embarrassing!"

"You're telling me!" They got back in the car and drove back to Louden. At the local grocery store, Page bought a cartfull of paper supplies to hand out to the whole apartment complex. She would make sure there was plenty on the truck they would send out next week. The stores were empty of water bottles; and when asked about it, the owner said they had already sent it all over to Smith Falls.

The B&B had supper waiting for them. They were exhausted and dirty from the day. A delicious supper hit the spot. They relayed to everyone staying there about the devastation, and all agreed to do something to help. Page and Chase went to their room to shower and change. They found themselves too tired to do anything but to turn in for the night. The emotions were still so raw from the day. They each went over a few things that stood out for them and updated the list they would take back to Johnstown. Chase said she was going to get a group of friends from the church to come out some weekend and help clean the debris.

The next day, Chase and Page went back to Ms. Yancy's and dropped off all the paper products. The people staying with her said they would divvy it out to the other neighbors too. They gave Ms. Yancy a hug, and they all prayed together before leaving back for Johnstown. There was going to be a community service later that day, but they needed to return home. The drive back was quiet, each lost in her own thought. They would occasionally share ideas, but the silence was peaceful.

Page and Chase decided to go to the Sunday night service at home, even though they were both exhausted physically and emotionally. As they pulled into town, they arrived a few minutes before the service started. This gave them a chance to visit with the pastor about what they found and give him the list of needs. After the service, they headed for a takeout place for supper and went home. They threw their bags on the floor and decided to unpack the next evening.

When Page arrived at work, she asked for a meeting with her partners. They were able to meet right away, and they all went to the boardroom and sat down with a cup of coffee. Page talked about the devastation and her embarrassing conversation with Mr. Cranshaw. The partners chuckled a bit at her embarrassment and shared equal embarrassing stories to try and make her feel a little better. Page told her partners she would like to donate her hours for the planning of a new healthcare facility. She knew legally there had to be charges for some of it, but any hours she spent she personally would donate as in-kind. The partners agreed it would be fine to do so, but to keep track of the hours; so they could document the in-kind donation appropriately. That is, if she got the job in the first place. Page was pleased, and they went on to discuss their weekly plans before each went back to work.

After work, Page drove to a consignment shop close by and looked around. There were rows and rows of clothes in all sizes and styles. She asked to see the owner and was introduced to Sally Grove. "Sally, my name is Page Lemon, and I want to buy your inventory." Sally blinked her eyes several times and stared at Page. She looked Page over and saw the designer clothing she was wearing. "Am I hearing you correctly? You want to buy everything? Why on earth would you want to do that?"

"I want to load it on a truck and send it over to Smith Falls to donate to everyone that lost their homes." Sally began smiling. "That makes more sense. You realize I have no idea what all this would cost."

"I will give you a couple of days to figure it out. Make sure the clothes are for the right season, a variety of sizes, and include shoes. I will send a semi over on Thursday; and if you leave them hanging on the racks, I will buy the racks from you. You can replace them with new ones. It will be easier for people to go through them if they are still hanging up, and they could use the hangers. Is that a deal?" Sally agreed and said she would get her staff to work on it right away and have it ready by Thursday. Page said she would be back sometime Thursday to give her a check. They shook hands; and Page left, leaving a smiling Sally behind. "That benefits Sally and Smith Falls!"

* * * * * * * * *

Page continued to think about her parents and their loss. The guilt she felt continued to grow until she couldn't take the stress any longer. After having a war within herself for several weeks, she decided she needed to return to Smith Falls to face her past once and for all. Page had explained everything to Chase, and they had even spent a few days in Smith Falls on a cleanup crew. But it did little to relieve the guilt Page was feeling. Chase was going to be gone on a school project for a couple of days the following week, so Page took that opportunity to return to Smith Falls to attempt to make peace with the past.

Page called Ms. Yancy and let her know she would be returning for a short visit and would be stopping by. She then made a reservation at a local motel and told Chase where she would be and why she was going. "Mom, I know you have been thinking about your parents a lot lately. I don't know what I would do without you, personally, but your parents weren't there for you. So I don't know why it matters." Page thought a moment before answering. "I don't know, Chase, but it does. It could be because when I left home, I refused to have any further dealings with my parents; and I may have missed out on finally reconciling with them. You know how you have felt a loss of your father even though you never met him? I think a child always wants the love of their parent, even when it isn't available."

"Hmm. You could be right, Mom. I have seemed to feel that loss, even though you have always been there for me. I hope you find what you are looking for."

"I do, too. If not, it won't be for a lack of trying."

The following week after Chase left, Page took off for Smith Falls. The closer she came to her destination, the more nervous she became. Page dropped her things off at the motel and headed over to Ms. Yancy's for her visit. Once settled at the table for a visit and pleasantries were out of the way, Ms. Yancy took one look at Page and said, "You are here about your parents, aren't you."

"You always know what I'm thinking. How do you do that?" Ms. Yancy chuckled. "My secret. Let me give you the name of the pastor and his number, then I can explain where to locate your parents in the cemetery. Then, we are going to have a pleasant evening, you and me. You are staying for supper and a game or two of backgammon. What do you say?" Page agreed readily, knowing it would do no good to argue with her anyway.

The following morning, Page called the pastor's number she was given and made arrangements to see him midmorning. She then drove over to the street where her old home used to sit before the tornado went through. She found new construction on several blocks, including the street she was looking for. The landmarks were long gone with the storm, and it took Page a few extra minutes to find the right street. She sat and looked at the area where both her and Grace's homes used to sit side by side. Silent tears streamed down her face as she thought of Grace and how Grace has essentially saved her from a lonely home life. Page thought back on her life growing up and realized there had been good memories along the way. She just hadn't thought of those times in years as they were so overridden by the solemn times. She looked at her watch and realized she was going to be late for her next appointment if she didn't get going.

Page drove on over to Ms. Yancy's church to meet with her pastor. Pastor Younger was an older, tall gentleman with salt and pepper hair. He greeted Page warmly and held both her hands in his as they introduced themselves. Inviting her into his office, he had her sit on a soft leather chair; and he sat across from her. She explained who her parents were and spent a few minutes explaining how she grew up and that she hadn't seen her parents once she left home. "After the tornado, and I realized they had been gone a couple of years, I realized I should have attempted to stay in touch with them somehow. I feel guilty about not even realizing they died. It was very selfish of me, and now it's too late." Pastor Younger reached over and grabbed a box of tissues for Page. "You know, I see a lot of people who need to express guilt but don't. They carry it with them, thinking the hurt they feel is their punishment, and they deserve to feel lousy. I assume you are a Christian?"

"Yes, my neighbor, Grace, taught me about Jesus Christ and his forgiveness, and I became a Christian because of her leading when I was a young teenager. Why?"

"Then you know if you ask for forgiveness it is so. We tend to carry our burdens even though we know that."

"I know. I came to find out about my parents, and their last years before they died. I prayed for them with Grace and for several years after that. I drifted away from the church for a few years, but I never gave up my faith. It is stronger now than ever. The reason I am here is that I'm hoping you can help me know about my parents. Ms. Yancy said they were being counseled, and even though it is probably private information, I was hoping you could tell me if they had changed or not. They cared so little about me I find it hard to forgive them for not being there for me. Pastor, I was hoping you could help me find the peace I'm looking for."

Pastor Younger walked over to a filing cabinet and riffled through several files before bringing out one he was looking for. "This file has a few notes on my counseling sessions with your parents. After today, it will be shredded. Normally, after someone has died, I get rid of the files as there is no further need for it. I kept theirs and when you called, I knew why." The pastor looked through his papers for a minute before looking up at Page. He extracted one sheet out of file and started to hand it over to her. "I'm going to give this to you. You mother wrote it at our last session. Your father was also here, and he helped her get it all down. We will talk after you read it." Pastor Younger handed the paper over to Page, pushed the tissue box closer and left the room to give her time alone.

> *Dearest Page,*
>
> *If you are reading this, it must mean something happened to us, and we didn't talk to you first.*
>
> *Your father and I woke up one day and realized that we hadn't seen you walking in and out of the house. Neither one of us had seen you at the supper table. We went to your room and found your Bible and your letters to us on the bed. You had been gone for months before we even noticed.*
>
> *Page, me drinking my life away was inexcusable, but I will say that due to my dependence, I hardly noticed your father let alone you. Your father and I were reckless with our lives. And when I found out I was pregnant, your father felt trapped in a marriage he wasn't sure he wanted to be in. His job was very important to him, and he spent a lot of time at the office. He wanted to make something of himself, and I was left home a lot.*

And with a baby on the way and then having you squalling, I felt trapped in a life I didn't want too.

So there we were, blaming each other for our lives and taking it out on you. I don't know what happened to us. The years seemed to fly by, and then we found ourselves alone again. When we read your letters, the guilt overtook us. I holed up in your room for two days before I could get myself together. I kept reading your letter over and over plus I began to read the Bible passages you had marked.

When I came out of the room, your father had found the envelope that had Ms. Yancy's name and number on it for guardianship, and he showed it to me. We were appalled and embarrassed. Your graduation announcement was on the refrigerator, and I had never even read it. We knew then as parents we were complete failures. We called Ms. Yancy and made an appointment to see her. She is a wonderful person and got us up to speed as to what you were accomplishing in your life. We asked her for some help and that led us to AA and Pastor Younger. I stopped drinking right away, but did slip more than once. My sponsor is wonderful and helps me stay sober. I haven't had a drink for eight months now.

Your father wants you to know that he apologizes for never being there for you and for being so verbally abusive to us both all those years. He has been receiving anger management and goes to the AA meetings with me. We have gotten to know each other again and found out that what brought us together in the first place will keep us together in the future. I can only hope that we can find you and let you know of our progress to improve and be better parents for you in the future. We were too selfish when you really needed us.

Page, we are both sorry about the past, and we want you to know that you had nothing to do with our behavior. We take total responsibility for all of it. We missed out on raising a wonderful person. And without the love of Grace and Ms. Yancy, I don't know what would have happened to you.

To close, we want you to know that Pastor Younger has shown us Christ's love. And we accepted him into our lives this day. We will be baptized soon. We have asked for his forgiveness. And now, we ask for yours, even though we don't deserve if from either of you.

We hope to talk to you soon, but if you don't want to see or hear from us, we will understand. We don't deserve your love or understanding let alone your forgiveness.

God Blessings,
Mom and Dad

P.S. I'm giving this to Pastor Younger for safe keeping until we try to find you or talk to you. It has been very cathartic to write this, and I hope when you read it, you will understand.

—Mom

The tears flowed silently while Page was reading the letter; but when she finished, she began sobbing. Pastor Younger came back into the room and cradled Page for several minutes as she cleansed herself of the pain and guilt she was feeling. Several tissues later, Page gathered herself. She sat silently, hiccupping as she attempted to control her emotions. The letter had fallen to the floor, and Page leaned over to pick it up.

"I can't believe this. They were going to find me." The pastor nodded. "I never got a chance to baptize them, but they were saved. Who knew but God that a few days later, I would be performing a funeral service for them? You can be reassured they are with him now." The tears began once again, but they were more for the joy for her parents being saved before their senseless dying. "I was feeling so guilty kicking them out of my life and then not even coming to a funeral for them." "It's okay, Page. They knew. And they were so proud of you for making something of yourself in spite of them. Your mom mentioned your neighbor, Grace, trying to talk to her over the years about you, but she ignored her. When your mom found your Bible and letters and realized that you had been praying for her, it shook her to the core. It took your parents a long time to come to grips with things, but then, they had years to work through before coming out on the other side."

Page and Pastor Younger talked a bit more about her parents, then Pastor Younger prayed with Page before she left. He handed her the box of tissues. "I think you may need these today." Page smiled and took the tissues. "I believe you're right, Pastor. I'll be headed to the cemetery after lunch. I have a bit of guilt I need to shed yet."

Page stopped at a drive thru and picked up lunch. She didn't want to sit in a restaurant with red and swollen eyes and runny nose. After she ate a quiet lunch at the park, she stopped by a hobby shop and picked up several flowers. Page drove slowly to the cemetery and stopped the car. She looked out at all the stones, and a throbbing heaviness came on her heart. Page picked up the flowers, the directions to her parents grave, and her box of tissues. Page slowly wound her way in the right direction until she came upon the row she needed. She stopped, took a cleansing breath, and looked up at the sky. "Lord, give me the strength I need to do this." Page paused for a couple more minutes before continuing down the row. When she came upon her parent's stone, she was shocked to see her parents names etched. It all became so real to her. She would never see her parents again. The tears began to flow silently down her cheeks. As she wiped the tears away, she began to notice the stone itself. It was beautiful with a picture of the local falls in the background. As she looked at the backside, she gasped. "Loving Parents of Page" was etched elegantly for all to see. Page crumpled to the soft grass and sobbed.

Once Page could gather herself together, she placed the flowers she brought in the urns on the headstone. She sat contemplating her parents, thinking about the letter she left lying in the car seat. Too late, her parents realized life had passed them by. The only consolation Page had was in the end, they had found Christ and were going to find her.

"I forgive you. With Grace's help, I always forgave you. But I've been feeling guilty about not keeping in touch. And now, you will never know your only grandchild. She is a wonderful girl. You would have been proud of her, too. I'll bring her by sometime, and I'll show her your letter. You'll never know how much that letter means to me. It came at a time when I truly needed it. It seems to be God's timing. Truly. I love you both even though you never made it easy to do so."

Page sat for a while longer. She stared out at the surroundings and noticed not the headstones this time, but what a beautiful setting it was. Trees and flowers were everywhere. It was very peaceful as the sun was starting to dip behind the tree line. Page got up, patted the headstone and said goodbye to her parents. A feeling of peace ful-filled her instead of the guilt she had been feeling before her trip to Smith Falls. She stopped by Grace's site on the way out of the cemetery and also left a few fresh flowers in her urn. "Grace, our prayers worked. Thank you for taking time with me all those years ago, and thank you for the prayers you sent up for my parents." It was time to go home.

Chapter 4

The intercom buzzed. "Page, you have a call from a Mr. Cranshaw from Smith Falls. He says he has a business card with your name on it."

"I'll take it. Thank you, Jenny." Page grabbed the phone. "Mr. Cranshaw! It is so nice to hear from you. How are things going in Smith Falls? I have been so busy the last couple of months I haven't kept up like I should."

"Ms. Lemon, I want to apologize for our first meeting. It wasn't very professional of me." "Think nothing of it Mr. Cranshaw! I apologize myself. I hadn't realized the circumstances at the time."

"Ms. Lemon, I guess we both were uncomfortable about it, so let's just forget about it. The reason I called was to ask if you were still interested in bidding on a building project. We are going to start the process of rebuilding the hospital and clinic. The board of directors wishes to look at bids. I will send you the specifications by fax if that would be OK?" "Mr. Cranshaw! That would be great! I am looking forward to working with the Smith Falls community again."

"Ms. Lemon, we would be honored to have you. After you send in your bid, the Board will have you come out for a formal interview and a tour of the grounds. We have it cleaned up now and whoever gets the bid will have to start from scratch." "That would be fine, Mr.

Cranshaw. I will look for your fax and will be anxious to see Smith Falls again. I haven't been back for the last couple of months, so I'm sure the clean-up process has made a lot of changes." "You're right. Things look a lot different these days. We have a community spirit that doesn't give up!" Page chuckled. "I know, Mr. Cranshaw. Believe me, I know. The fax number is on my card. Thanks for calling. We shall see you soon."

Page hung up the phone. She felt as giddy just like when she received her first solo assignment. She jumped up and practically ran out of her office. "Jenny! Look for a fax from Mr. Cranshaw!" Jenny looked startled as Page continued to fly thru the office and into the hallway. As she danced into Mr. Gregg's office, she yelled, "Charles! I finally got the call!" Charles Gregg jerked away from his computer and stared at Page. "What in the world are you yelling about?" About that time, Oscar Fielding heard all the commotion and poked his head in. "Yes. Tell us what in the devil you are screeching about now!" Page turned and looked at Oscar. She saw the smile on his face and continued smiling as large as a Cheshire cat. "The Smith Falls account! Mr. Cranshaw just called. He's faxing over the specs today! I get to work a deal!"

"Congratulations!" Oscar and Charles said at the same time! "I'm so excited. I can't wait to show them what I've been working on!" Both her partners looked at her. "You've been working on a spec?" said Charles. Page had the sense to at least appear a little sheepish about putting in hours on a project they hadn't even bid on yet. "I know. I know. But I just *had* to work on it." Both her partners looked at her and laughed. Oscar went back to his own office and left Page staring at Charles. "Well, I guess we better look at those specs and see if your time spent is even close to what they are wanting." Page grinned. I will bring them to the next meeting. Thanks, Charles!" Charles laughed and waved her out of the office. "I have work to do and so do you. Skedaddle!" Page turned and rushed back to her office.

"Jenny! Did that fax come in yet?" Jenny jumped again. "Will you stop that! You are going to give me a heart attack! And yes, here is your fax." Page grabbed the specs and continued on into her office. She yelled back over her shoulder, "Thanks, Jenny! You are the best!"

Doug Reilly was sitting at his desk, contemplating applications for an additional accountant in the Southern branch. The intercom buzzed. "Mr. Reilly, there is a young lady on the line for you. She says her name is Chase Lemon and thought you might want to visit with her. I asked her what it was about and she said it was personal. I wasn't sure what to tell her, but I have her on hold." Doug stared at the intercom and his heart began to race. "Mr. Reilly? Are you there?" Doug nervously looked at the intercom. "Just a minute, Ginger. Tell her I will be with her in a minute." Doug sat there, staring at the phone. When it started to blink again, his mouth was so dry he didn't even know if he could talk. He walked over to the wet bar and poured some tonic water and came back to the desk. He downed the whole glass before reaching for the phone.

"This is Doug Reilly. What may I help you with today?" Doug could hear a nervous shudder through the line. "At least I'm not the only one ill at ease here," he thought. After clearing her throat a couple of times, Chase thought she might as well plunge forward. "I got this number from the branch office in Johnstown and said this is where you work. I didn't know if you would talk to me or not. I'm your daughter, and I only found out about you six months ago. I know you and Mom didn't leave on good terms, and I'm not asking for anything. I just wanted to talk to you at least once and tell you how to reach me if you wanted to. I know this is probably a big shock to hear from me, so I don't expect you to have much to say at this point, or at all." Chase stopped rambling and took a deep breath.

Doug tried to wrap his head around the whole conversation. "I don't know what to say. It is quite the shock to hear from you. And you are right, I didn't know about you either. And as I've been working through several things in my life, I have realized that it is my fault for not knowing. I have wondered, actually, if you existed or not. I was not kind to your mother before I left. How old are you? Fifteen, sixteen?"

"I'm sixteen. I'll be seventeen in a couple of months." "My gosh. I can't believe all these years have passed by so quickly. Listen, I need to absorb this phone call. Please give me your number and the best times to call you. I will return a call to you in a couple of days after I've given some serious thought to everything." Chase gave Doug her cell number. "I'm not going to tell Mom I called you. We talked about you, and I know how things were left when you broke up. She gave me the local number and said I could do with it as I wished. I think for now we can just decide how much correspondence we can handle. Is that all right with you?" Doug sighed. "I think that is best. I don't think I could look your Mom in the eye right now. We will see what the future holds for us first. I'll call you in a couple of days, all right, Chase?"

"That's fine. Thanks for taking my call. *Bye.*" Chase hung up and left Doug holding the phone to his ear. He slowly replaced the receiver and turned to stare out of his window. The sky was turning gray and looked ready to rain. Doug thought that was about how he felt right now. An emotional storm was brewing inside of him.

Chase stared at the phone. It took six months before she had the nerve to make the call. Chase had started to dial the number several times but could never complete it. She didn't know what to expect, but she had run several scenarios through her mind over those last few months. None of them went as well as the call actually did. Chase had set herself to expect a denial and a hang up from him, not a "I'll call you later" scene. Chase felt pretty good about the whole call and was anxious to hear from him again. She knew what he looked like because she had found his picture on the company website. She finally had the answers as to where her looks came from. Chase looked in the mirror again. She smiled and felt a sense that the missing piece of her life was found. "Now if I can just hang on to it."

The time frame for meeting with the Smith Falls board of directors was set for two weeks from receiving the specs. They were on a time crunch; and now that they decided to go forward, they didn't want to wait around. Page was glad she had been doing some preliminary work and was excited for the meeting. She didn't know who she would have to compete against but thought the ace in the hole would be her offering her planning time as in-kind to cut down on Smith Falls costs, and it would knock the offer out of the park. Page and her partners all drove out to Smith Falls for the bid and surprise presentation.

"Mr. Cranshaw, so good to meet you again. These are my partners, Charles Gregg and Oscar Fielding."

"So good to meet you." Mr. Cranshaw turned and introduced them to the board members. As they all settled around a table in the library meeting room, Page handed out their bid to each board member.

"I want you to notice on page four, there is an in-kind offer for my services. I had mentioned to you at the onset that I wanted to give back to the community and my partners have graciously allowed me to work pro bono on this project. They, of course, have not." Everyone chuckled at her last remark. "I have actually brought a presentation based on your specs. I know you didn't expect anything so soon, but I was here shortly after the tornado and have been back several times thereafter. I knew the space I would probably be working with. And according to your specs, I'm not far off. If you wouldn't mind, I would like to show you what I had in mind." The board and Mr. Cranshaw were excited to see something in print already and helped set up for the presentation. Page had brought hard copies plus a thumb drive for a computer. She wasn't sure what would be available, but the library had the perfect set up already for a computer demonstration. She and her partners answered several questions as they went through each slide.

After the presentation, which included more than what the board had even considered, Page stated, "We will leave you with the hard copies, so you can stretch them out and show them to anyone you wish. We will await your decision." The board members and Mr. Cranshaw looked at each other and nodded. Mr. Cranshaw stood up. "Ms. Lemon, Gentleman. We want to thank you for your bid and presentation. I know we were asking for a lot when we gave such a short time frame. And believe it or not, you were the only one that could actually deliver. Two other companies bid the job but can't work on it for over a year. We love the initial design, and there is no contest. You have the job." Page jumped up and shook Mr. Cranshaw's hand so long and hard he had to pull it away. She then went around the table and shook everyone's hand. Her partners chuckled and told Mr. Cranshaw she had been like a kid in the candy store since he had called the office. Page stuck her tongue out at them. Then they all cracked up, laughing. "Yes, I'm excited. I will do a great job for the town of Smith Falls."

"I have no doubt," said Mr. Cranshaw. "No doubt indeed."

Chase heard her phone ringing in the other room. She was staying at a friend's house while her Mom was in Smith Falls. Chase jumped up off the couch. "I'll be back in a minute. It's probably my mom. Pause the movie." Chase popped into the bedroom and grabbed her phone. She answered without looking at the caller ID, so it wouldn't drop to voice mail. "Hello?"

"Hi, Chase. It's… ah… uh… it's your father." Chase smiled. "Dad. I'm glad you called." Doug felt strange being called dad. "Uh, Chase. How are you?"

"I'm good. You?"

"Fine. Just fine. Hmmm. Well, this is strange. I had all kinds of things to ask, and now I feel as dumb as a post." Chase laughed. "That'sOK. I have no idea where to start either." They both laughed, and it helped them relax. "I think I should get your e-mail address. I would do better with that than the phone. Would that be OK?"

"That would be fine, Dad. I like that idea. Besides, I'm over at a friend's house and can't be on the phone for long. We're in the middle of a movie." Chase gave Doug her e-mail address, and they agreed to correspond frequently until they were more comfortable with each other. After Chase hung up, she smiled all the way to the couch.

* * * * * * * * *

Chase and Doug had been corresponding for a couple of months by e-mail and occasionally a text. Doug had insinuated he would like to get together with her the next time he was in town, but he wanted to make sure she talked to her mother first to approve the visit. It was time for Chase to talk to her mom as she was more than ready to begin a one-on-one relationship with her father.

Chase arrived home from school to find her mother engrossed in her current building project, talking on the phone and working out issues that had cropped up in the last week. Chase left her to her business and fixed a quick snack while she waited for her mom to finish. Her mother always put her first, so she knew it wouldn't be long before Page hung up the phone.

In true form, Page walked into the kitchen and grabbed a bite of orange Chase had on a plate. "How was school today?"

"Nothing much going on, Mom, but I do need to talk to you about something."

"Uh-oh! Sounds serious! Boy problems?" Page joked. Chase giggled. "Well, not technically." Page frowned a bit. "OK. Out with it." Chase took a deep breath and refused to look up at her mom. "After we had that long talk about my dad, I thought about it for awhile, then I did attempt to find him. I got his number from the local office, and he still works for them." Page began to feel panicky. "Go on. I assume you have talked to him." Chase told her about calling him and how they had been in correspondence during the last couple of months and how he wanted to come see her. "But I have to have your permission to meet with him first."

"So, I assume that means you want to meet him in person now." Page continued to have a panicked feeling. All these years, and she hadn't heard a word from Doug. Now, her daughter was developing a relationship with him.

Chase let her mom mull over the conversation. She sat and finished her orange but couldn't look at her mom. "Chase, I told you before that you could contact him. I'm fine with that. I'm just surprised he has carried on any type of conversation with you, considering how our relationship blew up."

"Mom, I think he has changed. But of course, I didn't know him before. I just hope he doesn't disappoint me like he did you. I want to like him, and so far, I do. And you don't have to meet with him if you don't want to."

"Chase, I have no desire to see him again, but I won't stop you as long as you both agree to meet in a public place. In case things don't go well, you need to be safe and be able to leave without any problems. Does that make sense?"

"I understand. I don't think he's a mass murderer or anything!"

"I know that, Chase, but when you see someone in person, you can read their feelings and actions better than an e-mail or texts."

Chase agreed and promised to let Page know when they would be meeting. She was anxious to send off an e-mail to her father and let him know.

In the meantime, Chase was working with her church group for a mission trip to Blue Sky, Montana. Instead of going to Haiti this year, they wanted to do something closer to home like they had done in Smith Falls after the tornado. To top it off, by remaining in the States, more volunteers would be able to go and the individual cost would be much less. The teen group had a few fund raisers previously to help offset the cost and buy supplies for their next project so much of their money was raised. Recently, Blue Sky had seen several days of torrential rain, and many people were displaced by the floodwaters. The teens and their sponsors were ready to go help build some temporary shelters and provide much needed supplies. Additionally, there was a group of adult volunteers going to help provide the heavy lifting during the building projects. Their plan was to leave on spring break from school and return in time for the first day of class. Her mother chose to sit this trip out and said she would work on the project in Smith Falls while she was gone.

Chase filled out the proper paperwork for her trip and gave it to her mom for signature. As Page reached over to sign it, she realized that Doug's name was also listed as an emergency contact. It gave her pause. She looked up at Chase and back to the consent. Page sighed and signed her name then handed the consent back to Chase. She smiled briefly and walked into the kitchen to prepare supper.

Chase packed lightly, having done these trips before and knowing they were only allowed the minimum luggage due to the amount of supplies they would be hauling. She and her friends were getting excited to go and were continually texting to make sure they had everything they needed. Page checked everything over and dropped Chase off at the church parking lot. The assembly of teens and other volunteers were impressive. Page planned to leave directly to Smith Falls after dropping Chase off, so she could check on the progress of the new healthcare facility.

The building project was going well and was ahead of schedule, even with the occasional setbacks. The weather had cooperated during the laying of the foundation and the enclosure of the building went off without a hitch. The facility was much smaller and more efficient than the previous building. With the changes in the healthcare rules and people not staying in the hospital as long, the emphasis was placed on outpatient and procedures. The time frame for completion was placed aggressively at a year due to the community having no current facility. Page and her associates had hired a team of dedicated professionals for the job and were on the fast track. In turn, the community made it their priority to provide the necessary products and services required to supply the project and additional labor to make it happen. The clinic would be built after the completion of the hospital. The physicians were making due in an office building downtown and said they would be happy to wait until after the hospital was functioning before worrying about a new clinic. The foundation for the clinicwas poured now and waiting for work to start in a few weeks.

The church group was finally closing in on their traveling time. Chase had been enjoying the changes in the scenery. The trees were becoming thicker, and she could see the mountains on the horizon. They were just coming into view of a river when the drivers crested a hill and everyone began to pull over to the side of the road. Everyone got out and they were stunned at the devastation they could see for miles along the river route. Chase could see how far into the fields the flooding had run. Debris was left everywhere for miles on end. Someone pointed out the remains of what had probably been a house or barn that had been thrown off to the side in a field as the river flow decreased. Several people were snapping pictures of the area. Although they were still several miles out of Blue Sky, Chase realized that once again she was going to see devastation surrounding her. The leaders had everyone get together in a group and pray for the people of Blue Sky and the surrounding areas, to lead them to provide assistance to those in need, and be good stewards of the Lord. They all returned to their vehicles and headed on in to Blue Sky, but instead of the loud talking and laughing, it was a somber crew.

Chase texted Page late that evening that their group had arrived in Blue Sky and would be staying near some cabins on the outskirts of a heavily wooded area that backed up to a large mountain. There would be four teens to a tent plus their sponsor. The cabins were full of displaced residents. She mentioned briefly that there was a lot of devastation but felt their group could offer some relief. Page rested easy, knowing they had arrived safely and were settled in for the night.

Chapter 5

The volunteers, including Chase, arose early the next day and prepared for their assignments. After a hearty breakfast, they were trucked to their locations and all given assignments based on their skills. Some of the residents staying in the cabins decided to come along and help, knowing that they were lucky to have a place to stay while others were in shelters. The area was on a rise about a mile from the campgrounds. The ground was flat and some preparations were already completed. Several port-a-potties were already placed a short distance away. No plumbing would be completed anytime soon. The goal was to put families in individual structures as soon as possible. Water and septic tanks would be hauled in, but the volunteers wouldn't be there long enough to see the finished products. All in all, there were over one hundred volunteers and an additional thirty people from the area that were bringing in the equipment and supplies from the area. The chosen area was high and dry and only five miles from the town of Blue Sky. The Blue Sky River had crested ten feet over flood stage and had wreaked havoc along a fifty-mile stretch. By the end of the first day, everyone was hot and tired and ready to relax for the evening. Meals were brought in by church volunteers from the Blue Sky ministerial association. Everyone ate their fill and even enjoyed homemade ice cream for dessert.

Later, Chase and a small group of teens spread a blanket out by the trees and leaned back to watch the sun go down and the stars come out. They talked about the day, giggled about the mishaps, and relaxed enough to get ready for bed. Everyone stood up but Chase. "I'm going to sit here for just a little longer and enjoy the quiet." The rest of the group left and said they would see her in the morning. Chase relaxed watching the stars and tried to remember what constellations she would find this time of year.

As Chase realized she was dropping off to sleep, she decided she better get to her tent. Rustling noises through the bushes made her jump up and start folding the blanket. The last thing she wanted was to have a wild animal find her. Just as she turned to go back to the camp, an arm reached out and clamped over her mouth and another grabbed around her waist and began to pull her into the woods. Chase attempted to scream, but the hand was firmly placed and she was unable to make any noise. She tried to kick, but the stranger was holding her low enough she could only drag her feet. Her heart raced and panic set in. Chase was unable to think of anything. The stranger had an acrid sour smell that turned her stomach. She was pulled farther and farther into the woods, and all she could think about was how she hadn't gotten to meet her dad yet and how much her Mom would miss her. As full-fledged panic set in, she fainted.

Chase's tent mates had fallen asleep as soon as they tucked themselves in for the night. They were never aware Chase didn't return to the tent until they woke up the next morning and realized her sleeping bag was still empty. A couple of them decided to go back to where they had left Chase lying, assuming she had fallen asleep under the stars. When they got back to the spot they had been, they didn't find Chase or the blanket. They went back to the chaperon and explained. She went to see the spot and as she looked around, she noticed some markings on the ground that led into the woods. The chaperone knew immediately something was wrong but she didn't want the other kids to panic set. "OK, girls, let's go back to the group, and we will see if she is with anyone else and if not, we will have to begin a search." They all went back to the breakfast area and notified the leaders. Every volunteer was called to the area and when they realized Chase was not among them, the Pastor went to one of the cabins and asked that someone call the Sheriff immediately. In the meantime, Chase's chaperon stood crying and wringing her hands. She continued to apologize for falling asleep before making sure Chase was safe in the tent. The group came together under the pastor's tutelage and began praying for the safe return of Chase and for her to feel God's peace wherever she was.

It seemed like hours before Sheriff Donahue arrived, but it had only been minutes. He was taken to the area that Chase had last been seen. He asked that only a couple people go with him so as to not disturb the ground. The chaperon and one of the tent mates showed the Sheriff where they had been lying on a blanket. The grass where the blanket had been was pressed down and he could see that several teens had been lounging around. The chaperon pointed out the tracks that led into the woods. He looked at the area closely, asking everyone to remain away from the area. He followed the tracks for a short distance. Sheriff Donahue was frowning as he returned to the volunteers. "I am going to call in a group of law enforcement officers, and we are going into the woods. I don't want anyone to go anywhere close to that area for any reason. Is that understood?" Everyone quietly nodded their understanding. Pastor Becker walked up to the Sheriff. "Is there anything we can do at this point?" "Just pray, Pastor. Just pray." Pastor Becker turned back around when the Sheriff turned to call in assistance. "Everyone, I'm going to have to ask that we leave the area and go back to the work we came to do. I know that everyone here wants to go find Chase, but we have to let the law enforcement do their job. And it won't do anyone any good for us to get in their way. There are hurting people here in Blue Sky and we have a job to do. We will continue to pray as a group and individually throughout the day for both Chase and law enforcement. Now if you will eat a bite first, please get in your groups. And let's continue on. I will make sure we are updated frequently throughout the day. If they decide they want to use us to help search, then we can drop what we are doing. Staying busy will help us get through the day easier." Everyone turned reluctantly away and back to camp to get ready for the day. You could hear soft crying and little chattering as the group walked off to prepare for the day.

Pastor Becker went to his tent and got the information he needed. He called Page's office first. When he found out she was in Smith Falls, he decided to call the law enforcement in there and have them find and notify her of Chase's disappearance. Then, he made the same call to her father. Chase had confided just recently to Pastor Becker about her connection with her father, but he was still surprised to find his name on the emergency contact form. Since he was living on the coast, he thought it better to contact him personally and see what Doug was going to do.

Doug's cell phone was rumbling on his desk. He looked at the number; and not recognizing it, he let it go. He had plenty of work to do and didn't need a telemarketer to interrupt him. When his voice mail notification went off, he shrugged. "I'm not going to get any work done at this rate." Doug popped up his voice mail and listened to Pastor Becker's urgent message to call him back. The hair on the back of Doug's neck stood up. He was aware that Chase had something going on this weekend. Doug called the pastor back and listened to what he had to say, which didn't entail many details since no one really knew anything at that time. Doug told the Pastor he would come to Blue Sky as soon as possible but to call him if Chase was found. After he got off the phone, he sat in shock. "I may have lost a daughter I haven't even met yet." Doug bowed his head and prayed for Chase and added a prayer for Page. Doug notified his secretary of his emergency, and she arranged to a flight and rental car. Doug headed home to throw some clothes in a bag and hurried to the airport.

Page was walking around the hospital in Smith Falls doing a last minute inspection. A large part of the building project was completed and the community would start opening the doors to some treatments beginning the next day. Some parts of the building not completed were still walled off for safety, but Smith Falls was very close to having a complete hospital again. Page noticed the car pulling up the driveway, hoping it wasn't someone that required care. She watched it park out front and then realized it was the local Sheriff. She stood there and watched him as he got out and looked around. He then started for the doors.

Page decided to meet him at the doorway. She smiled and greeted him as she opened the locked door. "Sheriff! Coming to see the new facility?" The Sheriff looked grim. "Sorry, Page. I need to talk to you about something."

"Come on in, Sheriff. We can try out these great looking chairs in the foyer." Page led the Sheriff over to the seating area, but he remained standing. "Page, I have some bad news. Chase is missing up at Blue Sky."

"*What?* What are you talking about?" The Sheriff passed on the conversation he had with Pastor Becker. "I'm sorry. That's all the information I have. Pastor Becker said to call him as soon as I talked to you, and he could update you. But he wanted someone here when you heard the bad news." Page sat down with a thump and didn't even notice the soft buttery leather of the chair she chose. "I've got to go up there. I've got to go now!" Page jumped up to leave. The Sheriff escorted her to her car. "Page, drive back to Johnstown and get a flight. Don't try to drive up there. And don't speed and get yourself killed in the process. That won't do Chase any good." Page nodded and barely gave the Sheriff's statement any thought. She returned to her room and grabbed her things and headed for home and the closest airport. She calculated what she had in her current bag and figured she didn't need to pack anything else. She spent the next few minutes getting a plane ticket and found if she didn't stop between Smith Falls and the airport, she could make the flight. She'd worry about a car later. Once that was done, she called Pastor Becker and got an update, which meant she didn't learn anything new. But she let him know she would be there late that evening and to call if anything new came up. Pastor Becker prayed with Page before they hung up. Page called her office and let them know she was headed for Blue Sky and would stay in touch.

* * * * * * * * *

Chase woke up and found one of her wrists tied to a wooden beam. The blanket she had been using under the trees was wrapped around her and she was lying down. She didn't know if she fainted, fallen asleep, or both. She tried to think back to what happened. Chase remembered being dragged backward for a long time but everything after that was blank. She felt her body and realized she remained dressed, which was a relief. Chase was stiff and sore, but she thought it was from working so hard that day at the construction site and then being pulled along. Chase lifted her head and looked around. It was pitch black and even after attempting to adjust to the darkness, she couldn't make anything out. She listened to her surroundings and realized there was someone sleeping not far from her. The steady in and out breath sounds were more comforting than frightening because even though she knew she was in trouble, the unknown darkness was terrifying. Chase could hear and feel a slight cool breeze occasionally brush her face. She felt around her and realized she was lying on a bed of cedar boughs. Chase laid back and settled herself again. She reached to her back pocket and found her cell phone. Turning over and covering herself tightly with her blanket, she looked at the screen. The phone mocked her by saying it was searching for a signal. She looked at the battery icon and realized it was almost dead so she quickly shut it off to save the battery. Chase smiled at her one glimmer of hope. She knew that law enforcement could follow the pings of her phone and it would help locate her. Chase began to feel tired again and decided she was going to need her rest to deal with whatever the next day brought. She moved around and settled in for the night, which was difficult with one wrist tied. Saying a quick prayer, she felt a wave of peace come over her. Chase felt loved and safe, even with the danger sleeping just feet from her.

Chase awakened to the rattling of pans. She didn't want to move and let anyone know she was awake. Getting her bearings, she carefully opened one eye enough to see around her. She could see someone in the shadows, working over a small fire. Opening her eyes more, she looked around the room. It looked like a cave of some sort. Daylight was streaming in a small opening and the smoke from the fire was filtering up through an opening above. The beam she was tied to was sturdy, the walls of the cave smooth. It suddenly dawned on Chase that this was one of those old mines that the locals were talking about yesterday.

"You finally decided to wake up? About time." Chase was startled by the sudden arrival of her captor. The smell overtook her once again, and she became nauseated. She brought the blanket up around her nose. After lying on the cedar boughs, the cedar scent had embedded into the blanket. "Becky, I said get up. We've got things to do!"

Chase sat up, continuing to hold the blanket over her nose. "I need to go to the bathroom."

"That there pot will do the trick." Chase looked behind her and saw a large kettle. "You expect me to use that?"

"What's a matter with you, Becky? You always use that! Now get yourself relieved and get over here for a biscuit. We need to go find some berries and check my traps. The weather is going to turn, and we need to get us something to eat." Chase decided she didn't want to start the day upsetting her captor. As she made her way to the kettle, she puzzled over who Becky was. Clearly, there was a mistaken identity problem, but what to do about it was beyond Chase's thought process this morning.

Once the hard biscuits were gone, the captor took her rope and tied it to his waist. "You aren't going to run this time. You always get hurt running. You gotta learn it's dangerous out there." He picked up a pistol, a backpack, and a bucket and headed toward the opening of the mine. Chase had no choice but to go with him. The fresh air felt good, and she no longer had to smell the captor's filth. "What's your name? I need to know what to call you." The captor looked back at her briefly with a confused look. "You must have really bumped your head, Becky. You know my name." Chase continued to follow. "Um, yea. I bumped my head. So could you remind me what your name is?" The captor laughed long and hard. When he realized that Chase was serious, he said, "It's Mark. Can't you remember my name is Mark?" Chase played along. "Yea. Mark. I forgot. So Mark, I've forgotten a lot of things. Like, why do you have me tied up and why are we staying in a mine? I have a headache right now, and it hurts out here in the sunlight. I'm sorry I can't remember stuff." Mark stopped and looked back at Chase. He studied her face for a while and then turned back to the path. Chase started to pray again. "Please, Lord, place an army of angels around me."

The indistinct path led to a large berry patch. Mark set the bucket down by the bushes and then lowered himself on a large boulder. He continued to study Chase until she became nervous and started to fidget. "Becky, sit down for awhile and rest. You do look a mite peaked." Chase made her way to a boulder downwind from Mark's smell. Mark continued to watch her. "Becky. This is the deal. You fell and hit your head when you ran off one day. You got mad at me and wanted to go to our old home. I told you we couldn't return, and you left anyway. I told you to be careful but you fell and hit your head and you bled and bled. I thought for sure I lost you. Then, I find you sitting on a blanket and you looked like you were feeling OK again, so I drug you back with me where you belong. Now I gotta tie you up until I can trust you again. I gotta keep you safe. You understand?" Chase nodded as she tried to understand the predicament she was in. All she knew was that she had to cooperate to stay alive.

It suddenly dawned on her she hadn't turned her phone on. "Can I pick berries now? I'd like to eat some too. I'm still hungry."

"Sure. Go on. I'll sit here and keep an eye out for bears and cougars." Chase looked around and Mark chuckled. Chase grabbed the bucket and picked her way into the thicket, only being able to go as far as the rope would allow. She slipped her phone out of her pocket and turned it on. She was so grateful that it had previously been set to silence for the trip. Chase gave it a couple of minutes and then peeked at the screen. Searching. "How far from a tower were they?" She shut it back off and felt defeated.

After picking berries, they walked along to the areas where Mark had set up traps. One had caught a squirrel so Mark gathered it up and reset the trap. They dropped down to a stream, and Mark pulled up a net. There were two fish caught in the net. "Good day for eating," Mark said with a smile. As they walked back toward the mine shaft, Chase realized she was lost. They had walked all over the mountainside, and she had no idea where they were or how to get back. Her head really had hurt that morning, and she hadn't been paying any attention as they walked along. There was no way she could run if she got loose. Chase looked up at the clouds that had been building all morning, and Chase knew it wasn't going to be long before they got drenched if they didn't back soon. She smiled when she thought that maybe a good shower would do Mark good, considering the smell.

Mark prepared their meals for the day once they returned to the shelter of the mine. Chase couldn't watch him skin the squirrel, but she helped prepare the fish. The fire in the mine was small but served their purpose. The wind had come up shortly before they had returned, and they had made it into the mine just as the first drops of rain hit. The draft did help clean the air of their shelter, but it didn't do much for Mark's odor. They ate their supper quietly and Chase realized how hungry she was. Not having a lunch except for a few berries and breakfast wearing off quickly, Chase was exhausted from the stress and climbing and asked Mark if she could turn in early. He agreed and tied her back to the beam. Chase lay down and silently cried for herself and her mother. "Lord, please help me find a way out of here." Chase laid there praying with her back to Mark for a long time before sleep finally overtook her. Mark stared at her periodically with a confused look on his face. He would shake his head and go back to sharpening his knife or tending to the fire. As the fire burned down, Mark checked the rope and then turned in for the night.

* * * * * * * * *

Page was standing at the rental car desk and becoming quite frustrated. "What do you mean you have no cars to rent? I need to get up to Blue Sky tonight!" The clerk was becoming frustrated with Page, having explained that with all the reporters and volunteers arriving since the flood, rental cars and hotel rooms were at a premium. "You have to find me something. You just have to!" The clerk just shook her head.

"Page? Is that you?" Page turned around. Doug had arrived and was standing behind her in line. "Doug? What are you doing here?"

"Pastor Becker called me, and I came right out." Page was already agitated, and finding Doug behind her put her over the edge. "I can't believe the gall of you showing up! I can't believe it!"

"Page, I'm sorry you feel that way. Listen. I reserved a car this morning. You can ride up with me."

"I'm not going anywhere with you! I'll just sit here until they get something." Page stormed over to a row of seats and flopped into a chair. She sat there, holding her head, looking at the floor and mumbling about how life was insane.

Doug went to the counter and arranged for his car. Once he got the keys, he walked over to Page and dangled the keys in front of her and said, "Page. Here. You take the car, and I'll wait for another one. It's more important you get there." Page looked up at Doug and stared into his bright blue eyes. The same eyes she looked at every day in Chase. Multiple feelings took over and then exhaustion set in. "I'm such an idiot. I'm sorry, Doug. This day has just gone from bad to worse, and I've lost it. I'll ride up with you. I'm in no shape to drive."

"You sure? I don't want to add more stress to your day." Page got up and stretched. "Let's go. We have over an hour drive yet, and I don't want to talk about the past or my life or anything with you during this trip."

"No problem. This way."

Doug and Page loaded their luggage and headed out of the garage. Doug offered to stop at the first fast food place and get something to go. At the mention of food, Page heard a large grumbling from her own stomach. "I hadn't even thought of food. I have no idea what will be available when we arrive, so that's a good idea." They pulled into the first hamburger joint, grabbed meals to go and headed toward Blue Sky. They ate in silence. Doug found some quiet, soothing music on the satellite radio, and they each became lost in their own thoughts.

"Page. Page." Page opened her eyes. "Oh, my gosh! Did I actually fall asleep? Where are we?" Doug chuckled. "You didn't last twenty minutes. I stopped to get directions from this guy in the gas station. We are about fifteen minutes out. I just need to find the right road out. What with all the detours, it might be tough; so I need you to help me navigate."

"Care if I use the bathroom before we go?"

"Nope. Take your time. Get something to drink if you want. I picked up a case of water to take with us, but I grabbed a cup of coffee for me." Page nodded and headed into the building. She was ready five minutes later with her own cup of coffee. "Let's go, Doug. I haven't heard from anyone, so I assume they haven't found her." Doug turned the car into the traffic and headed out of town.

They quickly arrived at the campsite, and Page jumped out in search of Pastor Becker. The pastor had been watching for them to arrive and was very surprised to find Page riding with someone. As Page ran up to him, he held out his arms and enveloped her and immediately began praying for Chase and Page. Doug stood back and waited for the initial greeting and prayer time to end. As Page stepped back, Pastor Becker shook his head and told Page that no one had heard from Chase and that the Sheriff had lost the trail. They had had an afternoon thunderstorm, and any traces from the initial tracks were now gone.

Doug walked up and introduced himself to Pastor Becker. He looked at both Page and Doug with a raised brow. "We ran into each other at the car rental place. What are the odds?" Pastor Becker shook his head. "God is quite mysterious in his own ways." As they were making their way into the campground, Page could hear her name being called several times. As she looked around, she saw someone running toward her. "Page! I am so sorry! You have to forgive me!" As Page grabbed the blubbering woman's hands, she said, "Nancy. What in the world are you talking about?" Nancy continued to ask forgiveness and hold Page and continued to cry despondently. Pastor Becker explained that Nancy was the chaperon for Chase's tent and that she and the girls had fallen asleep and hadn't realized until the next morning that Chase was missing.

Page took Nancy's hand and led her over to a picnic bench. She helped Nancy sit down. "Nancy, listen. Stop blaming yourself for this. So many things played a part. If you want to take blame, then we have to blame Chase for staying behind and not going back to her tent. We need to blame who ever may have taken her. We could blame the church for bringing her here. We could blame the kids for not making her go to her tent when they did. We could blame me for not being here to watch over her. It goes on and on. Circumstances being what they are, we just can't do that. Human nature wants to take or place blame. But God allows us to make decisions, good or bad. We have to live with those decisions. I don't blame you, and I want you to talk to God about your heavy heart. In fact, let's pray right now for you to have peace about this situation." Nancy's flow of tears began to ebb as Page visited with her. Nancy looked up at Page and realized that she meant everything she said. Nancy nodded. "Lord, please know that this situation is heartbreaking to Nancy and the church family. We know as humans we make mistakes, and we ask that you provide peace in Nancy's heart as we know that you provide grace and forgiveness for our sins when we ask it. Lord, thank you for being our support system and help lead someone to find Chase quickly. We pray for peace and strength for Chase, the search party, and the church family as we face a new day. In Jesus name." Nancy and Page sat holding each other for a moment until Nancy finally reached up and held Page. "I hope you will sleep in our tent tonight. The girls and I will help support you tonight."

"I would be honored to, Nancy. I will get my things in a little while, and I'll be there soon."

"Wonderful. And thank you, Page, for being strong for not only me, but for Chase. You are one amazing woman." Page nodded as Nancy walked back to her tent. Page didn't feel strong. Her insides were shaking like a leaf, and it was all she could do to keep herself from falling apart in front of everyone. She took a deep cleansing breath and decided she better find Pastor Becker before turning in for the night.

Doug and Pastor Becker visited while Nancy and Page were occupied. The Pastor offered room in his tent for Doug, and he accepted. Page walked over and Pastor Becker held both their hands and prayed once more for Chase and then prayed for God to show the way for Doug, Page, and Chase to find a peaceful reunion. The Pastor then walked toward his tent and left Doug and Page looking at each other. Doug finally said, "Page, this has been a long day for us both. We can talk another time. You need to get some rest." At that he reached over and pressed his hands over hers and patted them. After he released her hands, he walked toward the pastor's tent. Page watched him go and then shook her head. "This is just a surreal situation." Page grabbed her bag and headed to Nancy's tent. Page was met with a tentfull of Chase's friends and Nancy, all wanting to express their comfort and support. Page knew it would be impossible to sleep tonight, but knew she needed to try to get as much rest as possible.

Chapter 6

In the morning, Page and Doug remained apart during breakfast. Most of the volunteers would be headed back home shortly after breakfast, but Pastor Becker and a handful of retired volunteers would remain behind for support and to continue to work on the housing project for a couple of days. Nancy would be leaving her tent behind, and the men would be moving the tents closer together once everyone else was packed up. Page would be getting new tent mates by the end of the day. Sheriff Donahue arrived early with several other deputies and outside agencies to begin their search again. A dog was brought in to try and find the scent. That alone encouraged Page and Doug. Page got a shirt out of Chase's bag and gave it to the Sheriff. "We are working with several agencies, Ms. Lemon. I hope we can find her today."

"Thank you, Sheriff. We will keep praying."

"You do that, Ms. Lemon. You do that." Taking the shirt, the Sheriff left to talk to the group waiting for him at the edge of the forest. The next thing they heard was a dog baying.

Doug helped at the building site with the other volunteers. Page and Chase were never far from his mind. He would stop frequently and pray for Chase. As the group returned to camp at the end of the day, they could see the search team making their way back down the mountain. It was a solemn group and Doug felt deflated. The Sheriff stopped to tell them they followed a trail, but it stopped along a creek bed. They couldn't find any tracks after that and it was starting to get dark, so they had to return. The Sheriff apologized for not finding her but stated they would all return in the morning. Page and Doug looked at each other, and then, Page walked off to her tent. She needed some time alone. All along, she felt it would only be a matter of hours until they found Chase; and now, it wasn't looking good at this point. Losing the trail didn't help matters and Page began to shake all over. She crumpled onto her sleeping bag and cried unshed tears for the next half hour.

Doug followed a path to a clearing and sat alone, looking at the mountain. "Where are you, Chase? What happened to you?" Doug bowed his head and tried to pray but had trouble clearing his mind. When he looked at Page, he saw the woman he loved seventeen years ago. "What an idiot I was." Disgusted with himself, he walked back to the camp and stood in line for his supper. Page arrived at the same time and stood behind him. "Doug, are you all right?" Doug jumped. "Page. I didn't realize you were behind me." Doug noticed the red swollen eyes and realized they also had dark circles under them. "To answer your question, no, I'm not all right. Maybe I don't have the right to feel like this, but I am devastated. And if I feel this bad, Lord only knows how bad you feel." Page looked at him and saw the exhaustion on his face. She realized she must look as bad if not worse. "You want to talk after supper?" Doug paused and searched her face for contempt and anger but saw only remorse. "We are a pair, aren't we? I'd love to talk after supper." Page smiled briefly. "OK, I'll meet you later." They both dished up their meals and wandered over to sit with the volunteers.

As the evening was coming to a close, Page and Doug picked up a couple of chairs and took them away from the camp a short ways; so they could talk without interruption. They sat facing the mountain, deep in their own thoughts. Pastor Becker wandered over to them. He brought his own chair and sat facing them. "I expect you two need to visit, but I just wanted to talk about Chase for a moment." Page and Doug both nodded in agreement for him to continue. "As you know, Chase is a smart and mature young woman. I have complete faith in her acceptance of Jesus Christ in her life and that wherever she is, Chase is praying for guidance, comfort, and peace not only for herself, but for her mother. I don't know if her relationship with Doug has developed to that point, but it wouldn't surprise me. I know from Chase that you two have not communicated for several years, so I would appreciate that you only think about Chase right now and any burdens you are carrying from a past relationship not be hashed out in this setting. The time isn't right, but maybe you know that." Doug looked at Page. "Pastor Becker, I know that Page and I need to talk, and I think we could use a third party. When we do have that talk, and it won't be until after Chase is found. Could we have it in your office?"

"That would be fine with me, Doug. OK with you Page?" Page nodded. "OK then. Let's pray for Chase and peace and understanding between the two of you."

After Pastor Becker left, Doug and Page continued to sit quietly. "Doug, he's right you know. This isn't the time."

"I know, I know. I just wanted to apologize for the day I left and my stupidity. If you would accept my apology, I think everything else can wait." Page contemplated his request and thought about the last several years as a single mother. She wouldn't change a thing and had no regrets. "It's OK, Doug. I accept your apology. We need to go forward, not look back and think about what could have been. God has been very good to Chase and me." The two sat and watched the stars come out, and Page talked about Chase and special moments over the years. As the moon lifted high in the sky, they silently gathered their chairs and went to their tents for the night.

Page tossed and turned, trying to get comfortable. Every time she closed her eyes, she would see Chase and Doug together. They looked so much alike. She thought of the moments they had shared, sitting there, looking at the mountain this evening, and realized that she never did hate Doug. Her anger at his selfishness had died as she grew to love Chase more and more every day. She was grateful for Chase and just wanted her to return safely. Page turned over and tried to cry as quietly as possible to not disturb her tent mates. It was so frustrating to wait for another day to search for her again. She gathered her thoughts about her and prayed for comfort, peace, and rest for not only herself, but also the volunteers. "God, keep Chase safe wherever she is and let her know we are looking for her." With that, Page turned over again and closed her eyes for another long, restless night. Doug and Pastor Becker talked long into the night about Chase and Page and Doug's entering into Chase's life in recent months. Doug knew he had failed as a father and had explained to Pastor Becker he had been counseling back home with his own pastor to come to grips with the decisions he had made in the past.

After they turned in for the night, Doug became restless again and went outside to sit for a while. He sat under the clear skies and wondered about Chase and where she could be. He looked over at Page's tent and felt a longing for her he hadn't felt for years. It was a strange feeling, and one he didn't want to think about for too long. He looked back at the mountain and went back to his tent and attempted to get some rest. It was going to be another long day tomorrow.

* * * * * * * * *

The day began much the same way for Chase. Mark continued to call her Becky and spent several hours roaming as they hiked the mountain for food. Chase checked her phone one more time and realized the battery was all but dead and no signal. There wasn't going to be enough power to ever call for help now. Chase continued to play along and follow Mark willingly. She remained tied to him, and Chase attempted to get more information from him when he talked to her about something. "Mark, can we do a campfire outside today? I'd like to stay outside since it's such a beautiful day."

"I guess so. I haven't made one for a long time because the grass has been so dry, but with all the rain we had, it should be OK."

"I'll make sure to keep an eye on it Mark." Mark tied her to a tree close to where he wanted the fire pit built, and Chase worked within her limited reach to build something appropriate. Chase hoped she could attract someone's attention to the area with the smoke. "I've got it ready to light, Mark." Mark came over to inspect it. "Looks good. I'll get some matches, and we'll get some lunch started."

When Mark got the fire started, she stood and looked down the mountain. "Mark, where did you find me? Can I see it from here?" Mark looked up at her and then down the mountain where Chase was staring. "Let's see. It would be farther over this way." Chase looked to the left and saw a slightly worn path down the mountain. "Were you out scouting for food when you found me? It was dark, wasn't it?" Mark looked puzzled again. "Becky, you must have hit your head harder than I thought. You probably need to rest. Sit down while I get our food ready." As Mark began to prepare lunch, Chase threw a little damp grass on the fire to make it smoke and sat back to watch as the tendrils rose. Chase prayed that someone would see it soon as she knew Mark wouldn't leave it burn for too long.

Mark turned and began cooking their meal of fish. After the food was done and it was dished up, Mark turned his back for a minute and Chase took that opportunity to throw more wet grass on the fire. She calmly sat there eating when Mark looked back. He frowned at the fire but sat and ate his meal. "We need to make sure that fire is out. I don't want to start the mountain on fire." "Why don't you get some water from the stream? I'll sit here and watch it." Mark checked her bindings and then walked down to the stream for a bucket of water. Chase threw more wet grass on the fire and watched the smoke rise. She knew that once Mark threw water on it, there would be more smoke and steam, and all she could do was hope for the best. Mark came back and covered the fire with water, then covered it with dirt and sand. When he was satisfied, he untied Chase and he escorted her back to the mine opening. "We need to rest a bit before scouting for supper, and I'm still worried about your concussion." Chase walked into the cave and lay down on her blanket. Only time would tell if the fire had made a difference. She knew there had to be people out looking for her. It was just a matter of time and luck running into them. It was a big mountain and Chase had no idea how anyone would ever find her. Chase sighed. She did need the rest as she wasn't used to the high altitude and all of the hiking they were doing every day.

Mark stayed outside the mine and was resting against the outside wall. He kept hearing noises and it was coming closer. He remained where he was and remained in a relaxed position even though he was becoming anxious. Finally, two deputies came into sight and hollered at him. He got up and wandered over to them. "What can I do for you gentlemen today?"

"Have you seen a young girl around here the last couple of days? We think she's lost and we have a search party out for her."

"Can't say that I have. My sister and I have been up here for a few weeks camping, and we haven't run into anyone."

"Well, if you see anyone, could you lead them back down the mountain to help? We would appreciate it."

"No problem, guys."

"Do you mind if I get some ID from you? You say you've been camping quite a while?"

"Yea, my sis and I are enjoying the area." Mark reached around and took out his wallet and gave his driver's license to the deputy.

"Where's your sister?" Mark thumbed toward the mine opening. "Becky's napping. We hiked all morning, and we were both resting for a couple of hours." The deputy handed the ID back to Mark, and he headed back to his spot and sat down. The deputies took one more look behind them and continued back down the mountain. It was getting late, and they needed to start back.

Chase awakened from a dream where she thought someone had rescued her. She thought she heard voices. Chase looked around and realized that Mark hadn't followed her into the mine and tied her. She quietly got up and walked toward the opening, hoping Mark wasn't in sight; but he was sitting right in front leaning against the smooth walls. She paused and listened. Chase knew she had imagined the voices in her dream and was so disappointed. She walked on out of the mine. Mark told her to sit down and relax as they would be scouting for food in a short while. He was staring off down the mountain, and when she looked in that direction, Chase thought she saw someone walking, but then the sight disappeared quickly. She looked back at Mark, and he was looking elsewhere. Chase shrugged and assumed her dreams and reality were getting themselves mixed up. Chase felt so disappointed that her dream was not reality, but she was determined to find a way to let someone know where she was.

Mark grabbed the rope and tied Chase to his waist again. "Let's see if we caught anything in the traps. Grab that bucket, and we'll get some of those berries you like so much." Chase followed Mark along, looking at the beautiful scenery. Any other time, Chase would enjoy hiking the mountain with friends, watching for wildlife. She was becoming more aware of her surroundings and watched their paths. Chase felt that if she could just get loose, she would head down the mountain anywhere and would at least be away from Mark. He continued to believe she was his sister, and Chase knew not to try to correct him. He was content with believing she was Becky, and she felt safe letting him continue in that belief. Chase had picked a half a bucket of berries and was just moving to another patch when Mark tugged the rope hard and whispered for her to stand still. Chase looked up and saw where Mark was looking. Across the meadow was a small cub bear, roaming toward them. Mark tugged her again. "Walk backwards very slowly and don't make any sudden moves." Chase willed her legs to move and worked her way back to Mark. She noticed he had his gun out and was staring farther off. Mama bear was watching them closely to make sure they didn't interfere with her cub. "Let's go. Just turn slowly, and let's get out of here. She won't chase us if we just wander off and leave her baby alone." Chase didn't know whether to believe him or not but felt comfort for the first time that Mark had a gun. They began to walk as quietly as possible the way they had come and ignored the bears. Mark would occasionally look back, and the farther they got away from the cub the safer they both felt. As they walked out of the sight of bears, Chase began to tremble and began to whimper. Mark stopped and allowed her to sit and regain her composure. "We'll be fine, Becky. That's why I keep an eye out while you gather the berries. You just never know what might be sneaking up on you."

"Thanks, Mark. I appreciate it. I didn't realize you really knew there were bears here."

"Let's take the berries back to camp, and then, we can go another path to check the traps."

Mark and Chase had no further problems with wildlife that day, but they did get to see a fawn curled up below some low-hanging limbs and several rabbits chasing through the meadow. Chase continued to be in awe how Mark could trap and fish yet didn't see the reality of who she truly was. She was beginning to enjoy his company in a way since he was so nice to her and was also grateful that he wasn't out to hurt her. She knew it could have been so much worse. Chase continued to pray often throughout the day about rescue and her safety. She knew she needed to ask for guidance to deal with Mark and to find a way to help him. She didn't know what would happen to her if he realized she wasn't his sister.

The deputies coming back down the mountain that day ran across Sheriff Donahue and told them about the man they ran into up by the abandoned mine. After some discussion, they all decided they would return the following day and investigate further. It was getting late in the day, and they didn't want to be caught in the dark. The grids were almost covered, and an expansion of the search would need to happen if something didn't break soon. The Sheriff reported to Page and Doug that there were no leads yet and apologized for another day seemingly wasted. They were glad the weather had been holding to provide easier searching.

Doug and Page realized they would need to stay yet another day. The rest of the volunteers were wrapping up their jobs and would be leaving the following day. Doug had helped as much as possible to keep himself busy. Page remained at the campsite and watched the mountain throughout the day and mentally calling out to Chase. Many of the displaced residents staying nearby had been helping with the new construction, and others remained around the area providing day care and some schooling. Page realized she was mentally exhausted when she had no interest in the construction process and didn't volunteer any assistance with problems that arose. Page managed her daily tasks without thinking and finally fell into her sleeping bag exhausted that evening. Her tent mates were exceptionally quiet that night, knowing that Page had not been sleeping. The group met out by a dwindling campfire and held one last prayer session for the Lemon family before retiring for the night. Doug appreciated their love and support and would miss them when they left to go back to Johnstown.

Sheriff Donahue returned to his office that night and looked up reports of missing locals and cross referenced Mark's name. He came across some information about a couple that had been missing for approximately three months after their parents house was foreclosed upon. The parents moved on but reported their son and daughter missing. The follow-up report listed a medical emergency notification for the daughter who had fallen off a cliff to the rocks below by a stream and was called in by a fisherman in the area who had seen it happen. It took some time to get someone notified as there was no local cell service on that side of the mountain. She was flown out to a trauma hospital and had subsequently died from head injuries. She had a backpack with ID and her parents were notified. The son had not been located yet. Becky and Mark Peterson. Sheriff Donahue paused and tapped the report. Looking at the picture of the girl, he had a gut feeling he had the answer to Chase Lemon's disappearance. He called his team in for an immediate planning session. They decided to head back up the mountain first thing in the morning and find that young man again, and hopefully Chase Lemon would be with him. They knew where the mine was and there was a direct path to the mine entrance. It took more than a couple of hours to get there, but there was plenty of cover for them along the way.

The following day everyone awoke to pouring rain, thunder and lightning and the search had to be called off. Page and Doug helped everyone pack up after breakfast and said their good-byes. All the volunteers would be returning to Johnstown. Pastor Becker left two of the smaller tents for them to use. With it pouring rain, Page and Doug sat drinking their coffee, looking up at the mountain from one of the tents. Page had spent the day yesterday staring at the mountain, occasionally catching a glimpse of the searchers as they worked themselves across the mountainside. Helicopters would fly over about every hour or so, marking off their own grids. Needless to say, Page was quite distressed; and as someone who had control over everything in her life, she felt very helpless. She visited very little with anyone over the course of the day and turned in early. She was exhausted and didn't know where to turn anymore. Doug had spent the previous day working with the volunteers again, but he too was showing the stress. Pastor Becker came over before leaving. "You have been amazing through this whole thing. You two are blessed with the strength that God has offered and in turn have been a blessing to the rest of us. Keep the faith." He prayed with them that Chase would be found soon and that Doug and Page could continue to find peace between them. Doug reached over and held Page's hand in his. "He's right, you have been awesome. I'm so glad to have gotten to know you again." At that, Doug walked off to help everyone get the cars packed and on their way. Page and Doug waved to everyone as they left and turned to look at the mountain again.

With the pouring rain, Page and Doug had little to occupy their time with. Knowing there wasn't a search going on that day, they chose to go to town and pick up a few supplies. They had gotten drenched this morning and on their list was some rain gear. "And coffee. Lots of coffee." Doug heartily agreed with that, and they ran to the car. They were quiet on the drive down. "Do you think the weather will clear today?"

"I don't know, Page. It doesn't look like it. We probably should check out the weather report. Do you want to stop somewhere and get a shower? I think there was a truck stop along the interstate."

"I got drenched this morning in the rain. I'll pass on the shower. Besides, I didn't bring anything to change into, and I'm not much into spending time shopping for anything but slickers." Doug looked over at Page as she was finger combing her hair as it dried. His heart went out to her, knowing that being away from the mountain even for an hour or so was difficult for her. Not having a search day was killing her. "Let's pick up a book or something to bide our time today. We won't have anything else to do except stare at each other."

"Whatever. Let's just get stuff and get back up there. I know it won't help, I just can't stand it." Doug nodded and pulled into a mini mall where they could get everything they needed. "I'm going to stop and get a hot meal before we go back. You have a preference?"

"I don't have a preference. But somewhere, I can get a big bowl of soup, and a sandwich would be fine." Once their stomachs were sated, Doug headed the car back to the mountain but stopped before they had driven a couple of blocks. "I'm going to check on room availability. We need something more than a tent if we have to stay too long." With that, he jumped out and ran into the motel. When he got back in the car, he said it would be a day or two before the reporters would all be leaving. Some were hanging around for a while to report on Chase, but the majority had been sent here to cover the flood and needed to head back. Page nodded as Doug headed back to camp. He pulled in as close as possible to their tents which were positioned under large conifers. It helped protect the tents from being blown away and the ground sloped away so the tent floors would remain dry. "Let's put the food in my tent since it's bigger. Do you need any help with your things?"

"No, I'm good. I think I will settle in for the afternoon and watch the mountain and the weather. Maybe read a bit."

"OK. Sounds good. Since the weather report said this would keep up all day, I guess we might as well call it a day. I'll see you later." Both headed out into the rain and directly into their tents with all their packages under their slickers.

As night began to fall, Page ran over to Doug's tent and sat down in a rush. "It's miserable out there. I'm going to have to put on an extra sweat shirt tonight."

"I know. Miserable may be too nice a word for it. Ready for a bite to eat?"

"Yea, I'm hungry. I thought we could grab some of that deli meat for sandwiches since I had a big lunch."

"Sounds good." They set to making up their own sandwiches and sat back for a quiet meal. All you could hear was the storm raging outside and munching of chips inside. After cleaning up and stashing everything in the cooler, Page said good night and headed back to her tent. She zipped the tent up tight to keep the cold wind and rain out and threw on an extra layer of clothes before crawling into the sleeping bag. She was happy she had a cot to keep her off the ground. It had gotten too dark to read, so she laid there listening to the storm and praying for Chase. She didn't even realize she was drifting off to sleep. Doug watched as she closed her tent up, sighed, and then did the same thing. Doug sat in one of the chairs, staring at the inside of his tent. He was restless, yet there was nothing he could do in this small space. He reorganized the tent to give himself a little more room for his sleeping bag then settled himself in. It was going to be a long night.

* * * * * * * * *

Mark and Chase sat staring out the mine opening. There was nothing they could do in the pouring rain. They were unable to check traps or gather berries. Mark did have some cans of supplies that they could use, but he was concerned how long the storm would last. Their supplies were only meant to be used if the traps were empty. He didn't want to go back to town, and it was a long hike. By noon, the storm continued to rage; so Mark reluctantly went to the supplies and looked them over. "Becky, do you want beans or sardines?"

"Gross, Mark. Sardines? Are you serious? I'll take the beans!" Mark chuckled. "That's OK. I'll eat 'em. You can have the beans." Mark opened the beans up and handed them over along with a spoon.

After they ate their meager meal, Chase looked over at Mark and grinned. "What are you looking at?"

"Why don't you go outside and get a shower. You stink! And take that sardine can with you!" Mark looked at Chase and laughed. "I probably do. I haven't showered in a couple of months. I do have a change of clothes that I can use."

"Go outside in your clothes and get them clean, too. And your blanket. This place reeks." Mark threw a small rock gently at Chase and agreed to get cleaned up. He took his blanket and ran outside. He hung his blanket on a nearby branch and then proceeded to take his clothes off. Chase turned around, blushing. "I better clean up in here a bit too." Chase took the bucket they used for a toilet and set it out the door without looking at Mark. She hoped he would get the hint and clean it up too. She then reorganized a few things to kill time while Mark was still outside. She noticed it was considerably better smelling already. She sat down on her cedar boughs with her back to the mine opening. When Mark was back, she was going to ask if she could stick her head out and wash her hair. It was matted down and a tangled mess.

Mark ran back into the mine laughing. "You were right. I stank. I left my clothes hanging in a tree for now. I'll go grab them after a while. I'll need to start a fire and get warmed up."

"You get dressed. I can work on the fire." Chase moved over to the fire pit and kept her head down while Mark was dressing. "Mark, do you care if I stick my head out and wash my hair? I won't go running off. The weather is miserable, and I have no desire to go out there and freeze like you did." Mark considered the suggestion for a bit. "As long as you just get your hair wet. I don't want you out in that rain. You still haven't recovered from your concussion, and I don't need you getting sick on me." Chase nodded her head. "Thanks, Mark." Chase went outside far enough to get her hair soaking wet. Although most of the rest of her got plenty wet too, she was glad to clean some of the grime off her. She returned to the fire and sat close enough to start drying off her clothes. Mark was fully dressed and had found another blanket for him to use for the night. "I think it's going to be cold tonight. We better throw some coal on the fire for the night and pull ourselves closer to the pit. This weather doesn't look like it's going to give up today." Mark waited for a short break in the weather and ran out to retrieve his clothes and blanket. He dropped them inside the opening in a sopping mess. "The water is pouring down the mountain. I wouldn't be surprised if there was another flood. I watched the last one rumble down the mountain. It was so loud I thought a train was going through. And I'll have to reset new traps in the creek bed. What a nuisance." Mark and Chase talked about the flooding and how he had to wait the rain out inside the mine for three days. "You were probably glad you didn't have to put up with me then. Wherever you were during your concussion, you were probably high and dry." Chase tried to come up with something to say. She didn't want to get him more confused. "I guess so, Mark. I really don't remember."

"Like I said, Becky, you aren't over that concussion yet." Chase just nodded. She sat staring out the entrance at the storm and kept fluffing her hair. It was almost dry. "It's getting dark. I'm going to move my stuff closer to the fire before I can't see to do it." Mark did the same thing, then threw some coal on the glowing embers. He wanted the fire pit to send out a little warmth most of the night, and he didn't want to use his firewood up. It was going to be a few days before he would be able to find anything dry enough to burn again.

The following morning, the rain had stopped, the sun was out, and Mark knew they would have to hike to a small store down the mountain to get supplies. They had eaten all the canned items they had and were getting low on coal. "Let's go to the store. It's a long walk, but they have anything we might need."

"Can I get a small bottle of shampoo to use?"

"Sure, but we have to clean this place out and hide our goods. If someone comes by, I don't want them to help themselves to my stuff." The two worked on picking up their personal items and tucked everything in a crevice behind the mine shaft. Then, they began to work their way down the mountain, starting out on top of the rocks and gradually on to a path that Chase hadn't used before. Mark was no longer tying Chase with the rope, and it made it easier for Chase to hike. Mark stated the trail took them to a small convenience store that hikers and hunters used. The people that ran it stayed in the hideaway store away from the general public, but they had electricity and a phone service for emergencies. Chase mulled that information over and contemplated how to get word out about her capture without Mark seeing or hearing her.

It took over four hours to hike to the Carefree Hideaway. Chase was getting hot, tired, and thirsty. She was ready to stop for a while. Mark led her into the store, and they walked around with a basket, picking up small cans of goods. Mark would haul them back in his backpack, so they had to be careful what they picked out. Mark had an extra small backpack that Chase was using, and she would pack a small bag of charcoal in it for the return trip. As Mark was looking at trapping items, Chase said she was going to look for a small bottle of shampoo and some toilet paper. Mark just nodded as he was thoroughly engrossed in the trapping supplies. Chase wandered over to the toiletries section and looked for a trial size bottle of shampoo. She didn't want to haul anything heavier than the coal back up the mountain. After finding what she needed and picked up a small package of toilet paper, she walked back over to Mark. He was also done shopping. He got out his wallet, and they walked over to the counter. "They have a snack shop in the next room, so we'll get a bite to eat and drink while we're here." Chase looked over at a doorway she hadn't noticed. The sign above it invited people in for a quick meal. Mark and Chase packed their items in the backpacks and walked into the small café. The options were limited to a few sandwiches, but there were several different drinks to choose from.

After sitting down to a couple of roast beef sandwiches and chips, they drank down two glasses of iced tea before they finished their meals. "I'll get us both a drink for the trip back. What do you want?"

"Just get some water." Chase looked around. "I'm going to use the bathroom before we leave. It will be nice to use a proper one for a change." Mark laughed but had to agree with her. He told her he would get the drinks and then do the same. When Chase came out of the bathroom, she asked the waitress if they had a charger for her phone and handed it to her. The waitress, who was very unfriendly, told her that she did but it wasn't available for anyone to use. Chase looked around. "Please keep this and call the local authorities about it. Tell them I want them to have it." Chase fidgeted and kept looking for Mark to arrive. The waitress was unwilling to take the phone and said she had no desire to call the authorities. She didn't want anything to do with them. Chase pushed it back at her and said to keep it. "Please! You have to call someone about me! Tell them to go to the mine!" Chase heard Mark coming across the room, so she turned from the waitress and left her phone and walked toward Mark. "Are you ready?"

"Yea, let's go. I got our drinks and put one in your pack." Mark and Chase headed back out the door, backpacks loaded with items. Mark knew it was only a matter of time before his money ran out, and he would have to go back to work. But he hoped by then, Becky would be feeling better and could also return to work. As they turned to head back up the mountain, Chase looked back toward the café and hoped that the waitress would be curious enough to plug in her phone and see the messages that she could never send due to lack of phone service and would call the authorities about her whereabouts.

Mark stopped along the route and led Chase to an area away from the trail. "Look at this view, will ya?" Chase walked over and joined Mark on a ridge overlooking the valley. The trees were layered with a sifting fog, weaving in and out of treetops. Eagles were floating on the wind streams across the skies. Chase agreed it was peaceful and stated she had never seen anything so beautiful. "Let's spend the evening under the stars. We can make beds from the leaves and branches and enjoy the fresh air. Whadda say, sis?"

"Well, I doubt I'd sleep well knowing there are wild animals around, but it is beautiful and we do have food. It's also been a long hike, and I'm getting pretty tired. I'm game if you are." Mark smiled and prepared a campsite for them, so they could look out over the valley. Chase leaned back against a tree and alternately watched Mark and the valley below. Chase had learned to trust Mark in the last few days but she continued her need to attempt to find a way to escape. She thought back to the waitress Chase tried to convince to call the authorities. It was a long shot to expect the girl to call due to her anger, but she hoped that her curiosity would make her charge the phone and see the messages about her missing and being held against her will. She also knew those messages could actually go out once cell service was reconnected, but Chase remembered they only had a landline due to no cell service at the café. She hoped her mom would know that she was okay, but Chase knew that even though her mom was strong, having Chase missing could devastate her. Her mom had been through so much emotional turmoil this year. Chase had silent tears flowing down her cheeks as she thought of her mom, her friends, her father, and her life. Mark noticed her crying and felt unsettled as he watched her. He went back to fixing up a small cook fire and prepared a light supper for them both. Mark continued to have some niggling thoughts in the back of his head, but he couldn't put them into order. He shook his head and blamed it on the hike in the altitude. After supper, they settled in to watch the sun set and the stars coming out. There was a full moon this night, and it made Chase feel better to be able see the area in front of her. As the evening wore on, she fell into an exhausted sleep. Mark soon followed, but not before those thoughts kept intruding about something not being quite right.

Mark and Chase made it back to the camp late afternoon the next day and began preparing camp once again. They had remained at the new campsite most of the day, resting and watching the eagles. It was relaxing, and they both hated to leave. Mark said they would come back soon and spend another night if she wanted to. As Mark cut fresh cedar boughs for them both and Chase put their meager supplies away, they settled on making camp once again. Mark brought their hidden supplies back into the mine. Mark said he would try to find some dry wood tomorrow to add to their supply. He needed to check on setting traps and repairing the damage done by the storm. Chase continued to pray that the waitress would do the right thing and she would be saved soon.

* * * * * * * * *

The next day, the sun wasn't even up before the Sheriff and his team started back up the mountain. He let the rest of the search team have another day off to rest knowing they could take care of the rescue with limited staffing. They had a plan in place and moved with a goal in mind. They knew they had found Chase. As the sun began to rise high in the sky, the team was within sight of the mine opening. They remained quiet and moved with precision. The team spread around the area and stayed out of sight. As the officers got closer to the mine, they all noticed it was very quiet. They walked quietly to the mine entrance and listened. Not a sound could be heard. The Sheriff and a deputy continued up to the opening. With everyone in place, the Sheriff called through the opening, "Mark, are you in there?" There was no sound. They entered the mine quietly and realized that there was no one around. The fire pit was cold, and there wasn't a sign of any camping equipment. The Sheriff looked around in frustration.

"I can't believe it. I just knew they would be here." Everyone agreed that the deputies must have scared the Peterson boy off when they checked him out a couple of days ago. As they left the mine, they looked around and attempted to follow any path that might show them the way they went, but what with the pouring rain the day before wiping out any normal traffic, they still couldn't see any tracks of anyone leaving the area. "They must have moved before the rain. Do you think they are still up here?" asked one of the deputies. The Sheriff rubbed the stubble on his jaw line and contemplated the situation. "I have a gut feeling they are still up here. I don't think he is too willing to give up the mountain just yet, but I don't know where to look now. Let's go back to the office and look at our grids again. We may have to start from scratch." The team wandered back down the mountain slowly and felt quite defeated. The Sheriff knew he had the right guy but was frustrated in being two steps behind him.

* * * * * * * * *

Doug and Page were enjoying a quick cup of coffee to start the day. They were sitting out in the early morning sun, looking at the mountain. That's when they realized the search team was already up the mountain. "They must have started early this morning. Is the weather turning?" Page got her phone out and checked the weather report. "It doesn't look like it, but I suppose they have almost completed their grids by now. I just wish they could find her. A couple of days ago, I swear I saw smoke drift like it was coming from a campfire."

"You did? Where?" Page tried to point out the area but realized that everything looked the same and couldn't pin point the site. "It doesn't matter anyway." Doug stood, looking at the mountain. "I may join the team tomorrow if they let me. It's going to drive me crazy to sit here all day and not do anything. That's one reason I was helping to finish up the construction."

"I completely understand. I'm going to see what is left in the cooler for meals. We might have to make a run into town tonight for more food." Page walked over and began to tally up what was left. "I think we're good until tomorrow noon. Then, we're going to need ice and a few supplies."

"Well, I'm glad they left all this camping gear. I'm not sure what we'll do with it when we go home."

"I'm sure we can just donate it to anyone staying in the cabins or the new site. Somebody's kids will enjoy sleeping out under the stars."

"Good plan. Let's grab a chair and continue watch the mountain for a while." Doug and Page took their chairs over to a sheltered area and could see an occasional movement in the trees that they thought was probably the search team. "We should have binoculars, so we could get a better look at things."

"I didn't think of that. We can get some when we run to town tomorrow." Page looked over at Doug and sighed. "Let's hope we don't have to be here tomorrow." Doug nodded, and they both turned their attention back to the mountain.

* * * * * * * * *

The Sheriff and his team came off the mountain late that morning and walked over to Page and Doug. Sheriff Donahue took off his hat and worried it with his hands. "I'm sorry. We thought we knew where she was, and we went up early to get her. There wasn't anyone around and no sign of them anywhere. But I do think we know who she is with. There is a young man named Mark Peterson who lost his sister sometime back, and Chase looks an awful lot like her. I don't believe she is in physical danger with him, if that helps at all."

"What are you saying, Sheriff? That she is with someone who is delusional? I'm not sure that is helpful at all!" The Sheriff nodded. "I understand what you mean, but as long as he thinks that Chase is his sister, then I believe she will be safe. We just need to figure out where they are hiding. We're going back to the office to figure out our next step." Doug took the Sheriffs hand and shook it. "Thank you for everything you are doing. I hope she is safe. If it's all the same to you, would you care if I went up with you tomorrow? I'm going nuts here with nothing to do."

"We'll talk about it tomorrow, son. I'll see you then." The Sheriff and his team left the area and headed back to the office. Sheriff Donahue assembled his team together to work out a plan for the following day.

"The weather is supposed to remain sunny the next couple of days. We need to make short work of this search. I think what we will do is every deputy will take a couple of the volunteers and work their way in each grid. Look for anything we may have missed the first time. Since the rain, we will be able to see fresh tracks. If anyone sees Mark and Chase, you are to remain in place and watch them. We need to know where they are staying, and we certainly need to make sure that Chase is safe. I don't want anyone to approach him and alert him to our presence. Only take volunteers that will stay quiet and are familiar with the area. If you see anything and can report it without being heard, click the mike twice. Everyone will stop in their tracks and wait to hear which one of you found them. Be quiet, and no one else is to respond. The rest of us will go back down one hundred yards, have the volunteers stay at that spot. Then, the officers will meet at the designated grid. Here is a list of your grids. Take one and pass the rest around. This way, you will all know which grid everyone is assigned to. Every day, I plan on returning to that mine. I just can't believe they were gone. It's too much of a safe haven to leave permanently. Any questions?" The Sheriff looked around the room. "You decide who you want to take with you as volunteers and give them a call. I will take Doug Reilly per his request and someone find me two others and give them a call. See you at 6 a.m. sharp. Dismissed."

The following day, the search team arrived again at the campground. The Sheriff agreed to allow Doug to go with him and two others. He explained the grid search details and what their plan was. Page agreed to remain at the camp in case Chase arrived on her own. Doug grabbed a backpack and loaded up a few items, threw a cap on, and was ready to go. Page watched as the teams split up along each grid and started the long climb to the top. Everyone followed their grids and kept as quiet as possible. No one had any luck finding footprints or paths that had been recently walked on. As each team arrived at their destination, they clicked once upon arrival. Once the Sheriff heard six clicks, he radioed to return home. They all moved back down the mountain as quietly as they arrived. It was a somber group that arrived at the campsite.

Sheriff Donahue stated they would be back tomorrow and try one more time. The weather was going to hold and they would repeat the same grids again. Doug agreed to go with the Sheriff once again. Even though no one had any luck, it helped burn the pent up energy Doug was experiencing; and he knew he would sleep well for a change. He and Page talked about the trip up the mountain, and Page was glad she had stayed behind. She was never one to experience mountain hiking even though Chase loved to go with friends. As expected, Doug turned in early and fell into a blissful sleep. Page remained up and sat out in the night, watching the stars change and twinkle. The moon was coming onto full that night and it was beautiful to watch it come up. It was high in the sky before Page turned in for the night.

* * * * * * * * *

The following day, the search team arrived bright and early. As they settled into their groups, Page offered them all a hot cup of coffee and the last of their supply of donuts. It was appreciated by all as they started to line up for their grids. Doug prepared early to go with the Sheriff, having gotten a good night's sleep for a change. As they began their ascent, Doug thanked the Sheriff for allowing him to go once again then moved over to cover his own area. The Sheriff had talked to Doug on their way back down the mountain yesterday about Mark Petersen and his sister, how they were located a few days previous, and why he thought Chase was safe. Doug felt better knowing more of the story and could understand why the Sheriff thought they might return to the mine. If more storms came through like that last couple, then the mine would be a safer place to be than a tent, as he could attest to.

As the day wore on, they were all arriving closer to the top. Occasionally, Doug would hear a click, meaning some of them had completed their respective grids. Suddenly, the Sheriff stopped and waved at everyone. When everyone finally stopped, he pointed through the trees and the mine opening was viewable. He pointed at Doug and a couple of other volunteers to walk back down the mountain to their designated spot. The Sheriff clicked his mike once. As Doug and the others quietly worked their way back down, Doug kept looking back at the Sheriff. Sheriff Donahue continued to stand behind a tree and monitor whatever he was looking at in front of him. Doug had not noticed anyone or had seen any tracks. He didn't know what the Sheriff had seen. As the group arrived down away from the Sheriff they stood and watched. Eventually. the Sheriff walked toward the mine and walked in the entrance. He came back out and shook his head. He looked around then came back down to the group. "Sorry guys. I just can't believe they aren't there." They left the area, and an hour later Mark. and Chase arrived back to the mine.

When the Sheriff arrived at the office that afternoon, there was a message from a waitress that worked at the Carefree Hideaway and said she had a phone from some girl that claimed that she had been kidnapped. The waitress didn't want to be involved but the girl shoved the phone into her hands and told her to please call someone and that they were going back to the mine. The waitress left it under the counter and forgot about it until that afternoon. She plugged it in and found out her name was Chase and there definitely was some unsent text messages about her being taken. The waitress said she was with another guy named Mark. They bought supplies, had a meal, and then headed back up the mountain. Someone could come and get her phone if they wanted to. The Sheriff called back to the Hideaway and talked to the waitress and made sure he got the complete story. He thanked her and agreed to have someone stop by and get the phone. The Sheriff then radioed a deputy in the area to retrieve the phone and get a written statement from the waitress.

* * * * * * * * *

Sheriff Donahue and a new group of volunteers along with his deputies returned to the campground at the break of dawn. "Page, we're going up one more time. The weather is supposed to change this evening, and we're in for another storm. I'd suggest while we are searching you pack up everything and when we get back you move to a motel in town. From the looks of the storm coming in, you shouldn't be spending it in tents."

"Alright Sheriff, that will give me something to do to kill time." "One more thing. Chase was spotted a day or two ago. She is fine and continues to be with Mark Petersen. We'll find her Page. Just give us time. OK, Doug, let's get a move on." The team moved to their grids and began their trek up the mountain. Page felt a glimmer of hope at Chase having been sighted. She prayed that this would be the day Chase came home.

Page started to clean up their campground. She talked to a family in one of the cabins about donating the tents, and they agreed to give them to someone staying in the cabins. Page gathered up the trash from everyone's stay, took the tents down, and packed most of their belongings in the car. She kept the cooler out until she prepared lunch. In between, she sat and watched the mountain and occasionally would see movement. She prayed they found Chase today what with the weather changing, knowing it would keep further searching at bay. Page worried that the search would be called off if the Sheriff kept coming up empty. She knew that it couldn't continue forever, but the Sheriff was sure Chase was alive and well. So Page felt they wouldn't give up too soon, especially since she was spotted recently.

As the teams were completing their search of the grids, Doug could again hear one click after another. They were arriving at their final destination when the Sheriff waved them all down again. This time, they were watching him as they knew he wanted to watch the mine when he arrived close enough to monitor any activities. The volunteer group moved back silently and stayed one hundred yards down the mountain. Doug continued to watch the Sheriff. At one point, he saw the Sheriff stand stiffly and reach up to his mike. He then turned slightly and pointed at the volunteers to move down the mountain farther. Doug became aware that the Sheriff may have located Chase and didn't want to leave. Two volunteers each took an arm and led Doug quietly down farther away from the area. They could see other deputies starting to converge on the area, along with the volunteers arriving to stand with Doug. Doug was quietly circled by the group of volunteers holding hands, bowing their heads in silent prayers. Doug bowed his head in his own prayer and tears poured down his face from both fear for Chase and thanks for the volunteers surrounding him. The volunteers used the circle to not only pray with Doug, but to keep him from moving closer to the Sheriff.

The deputies quietly arrived to the area and stood behind trees and brush to hide their appearance. The Sheriff pointed out that he saw two and nodded his head. He was relieved Mark and Chase had returned to the mine. His gut instinct told him they would, and the Sheriff was glad he listened. He waited until they were both inside the mine, figuring they were probably fixing lunch. He waved over to two deputies to come with him and he quietly led them to the mine entrance. They listened for a bit and could hear Mark and Chase talking. The Sheriff nodded his head. The other deputies took their place closer to the mine.

"Mark! Come on out! It's Sheriff Donahue, and we need to talk to you!" Mark and Chase were both startled. Chase jumped up, but Mark held her back and placed a hand over her mouth. "Don't say anything, Becky. I mean it." Chase nodded her head. Mark walked carefully to the opening. As he looked out, he saw the deputy and Sheriff off to the side. As he walked on out of the mine, he tried to act casual. "What can I do for you Sheriff?"

"Are you Mark Peterson?"

"Yea. So?" "You told this deputy that you were up here with your sister. Is that true?"

"I guess it was him. I wasn't paying that much attention."

"So where is your sister right now?"

"She went home. Why?" The Sheriff was becoming more aware of Mark's anxiety. He nodded to his deputy. The deputy started to go into the mine. Mark jerked around. "Hey! You can't go in there. That's mine, and I didn't say you could go in there!" The Sheriff took Mark's arm and brought him around and started to cuff him. The rest of the deputies took that as their cue to come out from behind the trees and close in. Mark began to jerk around and attempt to get away from the Sheriff. Mark was pushed down to the ground, cuffed; and one of the deputies held him in a sitting position. The other deputy had gone on into the mine and stood looking at Chase. Chase realized she was looking at her rescuer and started to cry. Shaking, she dropped to her knees and praised God for her safe release. The deputy went over to Chase, helped her up, and led her out of the mine. The deputies clapped as she walked outside. The volunteers heard the noise and began to run up to the mine with Doug in the lead. The Sheriff walked over and gave her a long comforting hug. "How about we go home?" Chase looked up and smiled. "How about we do just that?" Doug watched Chase start to walk with the Sheriff down the mountain. He stood there and waited a moment. When he couldn't stand it any longer he said, "Chase?" Chase looked around, and her eyes lit on her father. "Dad?" Doug held out his arms and she ran into them. They held each other tightly for a few minutes, both crying and shaking. Doug finally held her away from him and smiled. "You didn't have to work so hard to get me here, ya know." Chase smiled back. "It's so good to finally see you." Chase looked around. "Where's Mom?"

"She's down the mountain, waiting for us to bring you home."

"What are we waiting for? I can't wait to see her!" The deputies and volunteers cheered and clapped then began the progression down.

As they began their descent, Chase looked over at Mark. "Sheriff, can you tell me why Mark keeps calling me Becky?"

"I sure can. That is his sister's name. She died a couple of months ago from a fall up here somewhere."

"That explains it. I must look a lot like her, and he kept telling me he had to keep me tied up for safety. He needs help to deal with his sister's death, or someone else is going to get taken like I was."

"We will let the legal system take care of him. Let's get you down to your mom." Chase looked over at Mark, who had his head down as he walked with cuffed arms behind his back and escorted by two deputies. "Mark." He looked over to Chase. "It will be OK, Mark. Wait and see. You will be fine." Mark looked back down and kept walking.

Page sat, drinking her coffee, looking up at the mountain. Just as she was going to get another cup, she noticed the whole search team coming into view. She blinked a couple of times before she realized that she could see Chase with them. She started to run toward the mountain, yelling Chase's name as she went. Everyone in the area looked at her and then at the mountain. Everyone followed right behind her and was just as excited. Chase saw her mom, running and calling her name. The Sheriff looked down at her. "Go on, girl. Go on." Chase grinned back and took off running toward her mother. When they finally met up, they held on tight, crying and talking over each other. Everyone caught up and began to pat her on the back and offered hugs of their own. Doug stood back and watched, tears flowing. Page finally remembered Doug should be in the crowd somewhere. She looked around and found him, waiting behind everyone. Page took Chase's hand and led her through the crowd. Doug and Chase looked at each other, blue eyes and blond hair matching, the same shape of the nose. Doug reached out and Chase came into his arms. She finally felt complete and safe. Chase turned back and grabbed her mother and continued to hang onto her dad. She was so happy to return to safety and hold her parents. She didn't want to ever let them go.

Page, Doug, and Chase made their way to a tent to have time alone. Sheriff Donahue met them there once he had Mark ensconced with the deputy's vehicle, ready to go to jail. His Miranda rights were given, and Mark didn't want to talk to anyone and requested a lawyer. The Sheriff asked that Chase come to the office when she was ready to give her side of the story. Of course, Page and Doug were to come along. He also asked that Chase be checked out by the local physician, but Chase refused, stating she was fine; and Mark had never hurt her. The Lemons agreed to come to the office shortly and Doug offered to drive them down.

Page made a quick phone call to a local motel and found there was a room available later that day. She reserved that for herself and Chase, so they could get cleaned up and catch up on their sleep before the long trip home. Doug wasn't sure what he was going to do, but he couldn't leave until he knew Chase and Page were settled. The three of them sat in the quiet of the tent and held each other and talked about the last few days. Chase reassured her mom that she wasn't hurt—just dirty, tired, and hungry. Once they felt their nerves settle down, Doug got busy and finished packing up their belongings. Page called Pastor Becker and told him the good news. Chase explained to her parents about her captor believing that she was his sister that had died and wanted to make sure that Mark received help. "I just think there has to be something besides jail he needs. He didn't hurt me, Mom. He just thought I was his sister, and he wanted to keep me safe." Page looked at Doug and back to Chase. "Whew. I think we need to talk this over when we are rested up. How about we head to town and then talk about it over a good meal?"

"Sounds good, but I'm not going to change my mind about him needing help." Page gave Chase another hug. "You are so special. We can't see beyond a kidnapper, and you see someone that needs help. I think we have a long way to go to meet in the middle, young lady. Let's get out of here."

Doug collapsed the tents and gave them to the families in the new shelters, told everyone from the cabins good-bye, and headed for Blue Sky. The motel had an extra room, and Doug decided to stay the night and get some rest. Everyone made plane reservations for the next day, took showers, and met in the lobby to get something to eat. Chase and Page hadn't stopped talking since she came off the mountain. Doug waited for them in the lobby and smiled as they walked toward him. There was a nice restaurant across the street, so they walked over and had a large afternoon meal. They discussed what they would do when Chase went to the police department later that afternoon. Chase was adamant that Mark needed help, not jail time. Page and Doug decided to let Chase and the Sheriff's office work it out. "If the Sheriff can change your mind, he's a better man than me!" said Doug.

Chase gave her deposition later that day. She refused to file charges, and Page finally agreed. They requested that Mark be given mental health care to help him recover from his sister's death. The Sheriff said that the state would probably press kidnapping charges since Chase wouldn't and that he would encourage the judge to make sure Mark received inpatient care. Mark's parents would arrive later that evening, and he felt they would be able to assist Mark in recovering. Chase would have to return at some point and testify at his trial. She would be able to reinforce the need for medical care and not jail time to the judge. The Sheriff again wanted her to go to the hospital for a checkup, but Chase stated she was just tired and that no physical harm had been done.

After the deposition, Page allowed Doug and Chase to talk as long as they wanted. Page walked down the street and bought everyone a light supper and brought it back. They finished eating and Chase and Page both began yawning. They smiled at each other. "I think we need to call it a day. Let's head up to our room." They cleaned up their trash, and everyone went to their separate rooms. Doug stopped outside their room. "I need to leave right after breakfast for the airport. They serve a continental breakfast downstairs. Care to meet me there before I take off?"

"Sure, Dad. Buzz me when you get up, and I'll get around too. What time do we leave, Mom?"

"About two hours after your dad, so that will be fine for you to have breakfast with him."

"You can join us, you know."

"I know. We'll see how I feel in the morning."

"Page, I'll leave you the car, and you can drop it off at the airport. I'll get a ride over."

"Are you sure? We can catch a ride."

"Nope, that's fine. Here. Take the keys now, so I don't forget." Page took the keys and looked at Doug. "Thank you for coming, Doug."

"Yea. Thanks, Dad!" Chase reached over and gave him a big hug. Doug grabbed a hold of Chase and held on tight. "I'll see you in the morning, sunshine."

"Night, Dad!" The Lemons opened their door and went into the room, shutting the door quietly and leaving Doug staring at it. He finally shook his head and went to his own room.

The morning arrived early, and both Page and Chase met Doug for breakfast. They ate quickly as Doug needed to leave shortly, and one of the deputies had offered to drive him to the airport. He kissed Chase on the cheek and told her he would see her soon. He grasped Page's hands. "You've done a wonderful job with her, Page. I'm looking forward to seeing you both again." He pecked Page on the cheek. Page looked up and noticed the police car sitting outside the door, waiting to leave. Page and Chase waved at Doug as he left and went back to their room to get ready to leave for their own flight. "It's been a tough week for both of us, Chase. How about we go home?"

"I'm past ready for that. It's so good to get showers and use a real toilet!" They both laughed about that situation because they both had been living outdoors while Chase was on the mountain.

Chase and Page caught their flight home. Page had called the office after they got to the airport to let them know she would be returning home that day. Her partners both agreed she should take a couple of days off to rest and recuperate and just be with Chase. Page couldn't agree more and said she would come to the office in a couple of days to catch up. Doug flew home and was exhausted from the stress of the past week. He smiled about finally meeting Chase and what a wonderful girl she turned out to be. He called the office and said he would be taking a couple of days of to recuperate but would be in soon. All he wanted now was a hot shower and his own bed.

Chapter 7

Doug arrived home; and after taking off an additional day, he spent the next two days clearing up work that had piled up on his desk. He had little time to think of how he felt about meeting Chase and Page. He felt an immediate bond with Chase, but Page was a whole other issue. He knew, and should have known, that he loved her now even more than he did seventeen years ago. During his counseling visits with his own pastor, Doug brought up Page often enough during the conversations that even the Pastor had asked him that same question. Doug denied any feelings for her at that time; but since meeting her again, he couldn't deny it any longer. It explained why no other woman had been able to convince him to have more than a date or two. No one stacked up against Page.

Doug picked up the phone. "Hey, Boss! I need a favor. Mind if I fly in to see you next week?" After assigning the next week's jobs, Doug had his secretary set up his trip for Johnstown. "I'll plan on being there a week. Make it an open ended ticket, and I'll do standby when I'm ready to return." He called his friends the Cheetums and let them know he would be coming to town and arranged an evening with them. Doug called his pastor and set up a quick visit before he left town. He trusted his pastor, and they had become fast friends.

Then, he dropped a quick e-mail to Chase and asked how she was doing. He hoped to see her next week as he was planning a quick trip to Johnstown and told her to let him know which evening would be a good night to see her.

Page had returned to her office and had been working furiously to get through her backlog of phone calls. She made several calls to Smith Falls to check on their opening and how the rest of the construction was going. With no fires to put out at that site, she worked diligently to get back to speed on new contracts. Her partners handled several minor details and had other staff handle many of the others. The partners told Page to take a little more time off to be with Chase for a couple of weeks. She agreed that it would be nice to recover at home with Chase and cut her hours at the office in half for the next week. Page wanted to make sure she would be there for Chase every day, and there were projects she could work on from home.

Chase returned home and stayed there for the rest of the week. The school e-mailed her assignments; and her friend, Jenny, dropped off her books. Her mom was at home most of the time, and they both spent time just being with each other, grateful for the togetherness they shared. When Chase worked on her assignments, Page worked on projects. Chase felt ready to return to school that following Monday, but Page promised she would be close by if needed and would continue to work less that following week. Chase was overwhelmed by her classmates on her first day back, welcoming her with banners and balloons. She was exhausted by the end of the day and was glad to return to the quiet of her home. Chase hadn't checked her e-mail for several days, so she popped it open while waiting for supper and noticed one from her father. She got excited and told Page he was in town this week and wanted to know a good night for them to meet. "What do you think, Mom? Do you care what night? I can't Wednesday because of youth group at church but I'm not busy otherwise." Page turned and smiled. "I think that is nice, Chase. You mentioned once you thought he had changed. I think you are right. We didn't talk much up at Blue Sky, but he appears to be a Christian man and cares about you strongly. He may need you as much as you need him."

"Thanks Mom. I appreciate your understanding. I'll tell him to call me, and we will set up a time." Chase took off for her room to catch up on some homework while waiting for supper and her father to call.

Doug heard a ping on his phone and looked down. He smiled as he saw a reply from Chase. Doug looked back at his boss. "And there is the reason for my question." Mr. Kerry looked back at Doug and smiled. I think we can figure out a way to work everything out. You have done a great job for this firm from day one and have never asked for anything. Give me two weeks to work out a transfer and the job here is yours. Do you have someone in mind to take over there or do I need to transfer someone out?" Doug had considered this option over the weekend. "I believe we have someone in my office you can trust to handle things. Her name is Jennifer Hanson. She reminds me a little bit of myself when I first came on."

"I'll look at her file; but if you think she fits the spot, it could make this transition pretty smooth. Now get out of here and take the week off. I'll let you know when you can come home again." Doug stood up and shook Mr. Kerry's hand. "I really appreciate this. You don't know how much." On his way out of the building, Doug called Chase and made a dinner date with her the following day. "Can I pick you up?"

"Sure, Dad. I'll text you the address."

"OK. I'll see you at six sharp!"

Doug drove over to the Cheetums for dinner and great conversation. They caught up on their lives, and Doug spent the next hour telling them about Chase and then the recent event up in Blue Sky. The Cheetums were surprised to learn about Chase but were thrilled that Doug was returning to Johnstown to be closer to her. He couldn't wait to tell Chase about the move. Doug hoped she would be as happy about it as he was.

The following day, Doug followed the directions to Page's place to pick up Chase. He hoped he would have a chance to see Page. When he arrived, Chase answered the door and was ready to leave. Chase yelled out to her mom she was leaving. He heard Page answer her to have fun then they were headed out the door. His evening with Chase went well, and they talked and laughed easily together. They asked questions about each other and managed to find out they liked some of the same authors, music, and art. As the evening wound down and Doug took Chase back home, he let her know that he would be moving back to Johnstown; and they would be able to see each other more often. Chase was thrilled and couldn't wait to tell her mom. Doug walked her back to the door and gave her a hug. "I'd like to see your Mom sometime. We need to talk now that you are safe and sound."

"You want to do that now?"

"No, but you tell her I will ask to see her when I get moved back. I want to make amends all the way around. I hope I'm not seventeen years too late. I already apologized to your mom and she accepted it, but we agreed to talk again once you were found."

"I'll tell her, Dad. See you later!" Doug reached over and gave Chase a big hug and a kiss on the cheek. "Take care, little one. I just found you, I don't want to lose you!" Chase smiled and entered the house.

Chase told her mom about Doug moving back and wanting to talk to her. Page told Chase she knew they needed to talk and agreed she might as well get it over with. If he was moving back, then Doug would be in their lives more all the time. Page didn't want any hard feelings to come between any of them.

The next few weeks moved quickly for Doug. Jennifer was promoted to his position, and he was free to move back to Johnstown. He looked around his place as he packed and realized he had never put down roots in the whole time he had been there. It was going to be an easy move. The place was on the market only four days before it sold. Doug had listed it well under current market value but still recouped his investment. He found an apartment in Johnstown while he was there and would ship his meager belongings out. The movers would arrive that afternoon and Doug was all but finished with his personal belongings. He grabbed his laptop and a few final items he needed to travel with and took them to the car. The van pulled up for the move at the same time. His house was quickly emptied, and Doug took one last look around before locking the door. He felt no connection. "The story of my life. I've never put down roots." He shook his head, got into his car, and headed for Johnstown. "Home. I'm headed for home."

* * * * * * * * *

Doug moved into his apartment and quickly organized the few items he had. He hadn't realized that even though he previously lived in a house, his furniture didn't even fill up his current apartment. What he had was comfortable, but it made him amazingly aware of his detachment to his living circumstances. He looked around the apartment. "I'm going to have to do something about this. Maybe Chase can help me make it feel more like home." He smiled. Chase. What a wonderful girl she was. Doug then chastised himself for losing so many years of not being there for her. He shrugged and thought of how he would try to make up some of that time, if she would allow it. Then, there was Page. Just the thought of Page made him smile. Maybe, just maybe, he could make it up to her too.

Doug invited Chase over to his apartment the weekend after he was settled in. Once he got her opinion on the state of disrepair of his furniture, they went shopping for some new items. "Dad, there is a nice second hand shop here that can take your used stuff, and then it won't go to the landfill."

"That sounds like a plan, munchkin. Let's go spend some money!" Chase and Doug spent the better part of the day buying some new furniture and wall hangings. They stopped by the shop Chase had mentioned and arranged for them to stop by and pick up his old furniture. Doug had bought more items than he had planned, but Chase was really into making the apartment comfortable. They also picked out an extra bed in case Chase stayed over at some point. Chase wasn't done shopping for the day. "Now we need to pick out some bedding for both beds. Those awful sheets you have just won't go with your new décor."

"Chase, I think you have found your niche. You are quite the salesperson!" Chase just laughed and dragged Doug into the bedding shop. By the time they left that shop, Chase had not only picked out new bedding, but also towels, washcloths, and dish towels. "Where does it all end, Chase?"

"With supper. You owe me supper for doing all this work for you."

"You're on."

After supper, Chase helped unload the extra packages in the apartment, and Doug took her home. "Mind if I talk to your mom for a minute?"

"Sure. Let me get her." Doug stood outside the door and waited for Page to come out. "Come on into the foyer, Doug. What can I do for you?" Doug came in and looked at Page. His heartbeat sped up, and his mouth went dry. He felt like a giddy teenager. Page waited patiently for him to say something. "Um. Well, when we were in Blue Sky, Pastor Becker told us we could come to his office and talk about our past, so we were on neutral ground. I would like to do that now that I've moved back."

"I see. I did agree to that. Did you want me to make an appointment?"

"I think it's time. Now that I've been spending more time with Chase, I would like our relationship to be clear of any resentment and reservations and see where that leads us." Page looked at Doug and blushed. "Why don't you meet us at church on Sunday, and we can visit with Pastor Becker afterwards and set up a time?"

"That would be great. I usually go with the Cheetums to their church, but Chase talks about how great the youth group is at your church. And after Blue Sky, I have a great respect for Pastor Becker and many of the volunteers that I met there. I will plan to be there tomorrow and meet you out front." Once they agreed on a time, Doug left for home.

Page turned and leaned back on the doorway. "What am I letting myself in for?" She sighed and headed back to the den to finish up some projects. As she passed Chase's room, she looked in and watched her chat on the phone and twirl her hair. She looked so much like Doug. How had she not noticed that all these years? Page waved at Chase when she looked up and smiled. Page walked down the hall and thought of Doug. "Tomorrow could be interesting."

Doug met Page and Chase in front of the church and ran into Pastor Becker. Doug mentioned they would need to make an appointment, and the pastor instructed them to see his secretary after church to find a slot that would work for them. They made their way to the usual pew the Lemon's sat in and Page could hear a few people whispering questions about who Doug was. Page had Doug sit by Chase and smiled at those around her. Page had timed the arrival to correspond shortly before the service started to keep the questions at bay, but she knew once church was over, she would have to introduce Doug to several people. There were many people there that had already met him while in Blue Sky, and she hoped that those people would run interference for her. It didn't take much to see that Doug was Chase's father. Most people should be able to put two and two together. Page was so distracted she realized that the sermon was half over, and she hadn't been listening. Chagrined, she settled in and concentrated on the rest of the service.

After the service, Page made it a point to locate the secretary and left Chase and Doug to fend for themselves. "OK. I'm a chicken," she said to herself. As the secretary loaded up the appointment times available, Page went back to rescue Doug and Chase from the multitude of questions coming their way. Chase excused herself to talk to friends as Doug extricated himself from the crowd and followed Page back to the secretary's office. Once the appointment was made for the following week, Page excused herself and located Chase to go home. They said good-bye to everyone and left the church grounds. Page breathed a sigh of relief. Chase chatted about some of the comments that were made; and Page half listened, her mind on the appointment coming up.

"Mom, are you OK?"

"Just a little distracted. We made an appointment to clear the air, so to speak. I'm a little nervous about it I guess."

"Dad is a good man, and you need to talk and get all that over with."

"You and Pastor Becker. Are you two ganging up on me?" Chase giggled. "No, but you can't avoid him forever. He has done nothing but treat me right, and we have a good time together."

"I know, honey. And I'm glad you finally have your father. I just don't know how I feel about things, so the appointment will be good for everyone involved."

Doug watched Page and Chase leave the church. He had his own mixed feelings about the current state of things. What did he really want out of this relationship? Pastor Becker was so right when he requested they meet at his office. His old pastor would concur. It was past time to clear the air.

As the time of the appointment came closer, Page became very anxious. She had always put the past behind her and moved forward, even though not facing her past wasn't healthy. It had been her way of coping for as long as she could remember. Chase offered to drive her when she realized how nervous her mother was. Page appreciated the offer and took her up on it. Chase arranged to go next door to the pastor's house while her parents were in their meeting. Everyone arrived to the church around the same time. Pastor Becker invited everyone to his office, but Chase explained she would be headed to his place while they were meeting. The pastor requested they sit down and proceeded to have a short prayer with Page and Doug for peace and understanding. "I'll sit over here and monitor things, but I want you two to start to talk about the past and work out any conflicts. Hopefully, I won't have to intervene. If I need to at any time, I will help lead the conversation, but I think this will go better than you hoped. I have complete faith in you two." Doug and Page looked at each other briefly. Page turned to look at the floor. She couldn't look into those blue eyes without a lot of conflict. Doug sat back and tried to think of his prepared speech. His mind went blank. He closed his eyes briefly and decided to talk from the heart.

"Page, I'm glad you accepted my apology when we were in Blue Sky, but an apology isn't worth much without action. I also need to explain myself and hope you can understand what an idiot I was, and maybe I still am." Page looked at Doug briefly in surprise. She sat back and tried to relax a bit. "Go on. I'm ready to listen."

"You know that if I hadn't had the Cheetums come into my life, things would have turned out quite differently for me. They led both my mom and me to Christ and everything changed. After college, though, I became quite driven to never be poor again. When I met you, I found the antithesis of me—both driven for bigger things in our lives. I had never met anyone that I felt so much for so quickly. The difference was I had walked away from the church, thinking I knew what was best for me and me alone. I was very self-absorbed and no one was going to get in the way of my goals. Page, you were the best thing that ever happened to me, and I let it go because of my greed. When you told me you were pregnant, my selfishness got in the way and ruined any relationship we could have had. I walked away like it was nothing, demanding you have an abortion. Guilt tried to interrupt my thinking, but I would just push it away and work harder. Moving helped, and I threw everything I had into my work. If I thought of you, I would just remember you telling me to leave and not come back. I would come home to see my mother and think about calling you, but I was too proud to follow through. I had women throw themselves at me due to my position and money, but no one came close to meeting your qualifications. When my mom died, I spent some time with the Cheetums and went to church with them before returning back to the coast. It wasn't until then that I realized what I had been missing all those years. I located a church and started counseling. It must have been God's timing because when Chase called, I was ready to be the man I should have been seventeen years ago. Had she called me anytime in the years previously, I doubt I would have accepted her with any graciousness. In fact, I probably would have treated her like I had treated you. What a callous and selfish man I had become. I'm not proud of those years, but I've come to terms with it and want to ask you again for your understanding. I wouldn't have made a good father for Chase all those years previous, but I can now. I know I can now if you will accept me." Doug looked over at Page and saw the tears streaming down her face. His own eyes had welled up as he was talking.

Page looked over at Doug. "Thank you for explaining all those years. It makes sense. I need to explain my past now, and you will see that we are both at fault." Page worked on getting herself under control before speaking. "I have seldom had anyone I could rely on in my whole life. If it hadn't been for my neighbor, Grace, I wouldn't be where I am today either. I guess we have that in common. You're right. When we met, the bond was strong due to our similar goals in life. I had just begun to make a strong showing at my job and had just gained my partnership when we met. When you blamed me for trapping you and wanted me to have an abortion, it was just one more person failing me. I couldn't and wouldn't abort my child. After my initial shock from your reaction, I worked that much harder. I developed a way to work as a single mother and still fulfill my job. Chase has been the best thing that ever happened in my life, and I was not going to allow her to be ignored the way I was my whole life. A parent has to be the most important person in a child's life, and I probably was a little too much so, trying to make up for being both parents. But she is a wonderful child and has never disappointed me, nor have I ever been disappointed that I chose to have her. We separated on terrible circumstances, and I had no desire to tell you about bringing Chase into the world. I felt that if you wanted me to have an abortion, then you excused yourself out of her life right then. I have managed to provide for her very well, and she is a wealthy woman in her own right. Chase will never want for anything. The only thing she wanted was to know her father but was kind enough to not press the issue until I was ready. When Smith Falls was devastated by the tornado a couple of years ago, I was an emotional mess. Chase came home and found me watching TV and agitated. I knew then she needed to understand my past. Or maybe it was me that finally had to come to an understanding about my past. I had tried to ignore it for a long time. So I sat down and poured out my life story to Chase; and eventually, we had the conversation about you. I had always kept your main office number handy for Chase because I knew eventually she would ask questions. Although I didn't know if you still worked for them, it was all I had; and she deserved to know about you, good and bad. I let her make the decision about calling you. It took her a few months, but she handled it like a trooper and was surprised when you treated her with respect. I had tried to remain neutral in my explanation of our relationship. You have been good to her, and she has become a happier person with you in her life. I think she feels more complete now. I don't regret her getting you know you, Doug. I'm just sorry it took so many years. Maybe it is all in God's timing, as I probably wouldn't have been as gracious before the tragedy in Smith Falls and me having to face my own past."

Pastor Becker spoke up at the pause in conversation. "Doug, where do you want this relationship with Page to go since you have been suddenly reintroduced to each other?" Doug looked at Pastor Becker then over to Page. "Page, I watched you in Blue Sky. You are still that strong person I met so many years ago—and more beautiful inside and out. I would like to get to know you better and rebuild that relationship that we started so many years ago. That is, if you will allow me." Pastor Becker looked over at Page. "Page, where do you want this relationship with Doug to go?" Page looked up at the ceiling. "I don't know. I know that all these years, I hadn't realized how much Chase looks like Doug. And now, every time I look at her, that's all I see." Page turned to look at Doug. "I would be willing to do things occasionally as a family first. And if the dynamics is right, then we can look into a more personal relationship. I haven't had any real relationships myself since you left. I threw everything into raising Chase, and I'm not about to mess that up now." Doug nodded. "I understand and would be happy to work with that. I think Chase would be thrilled with us doing things together." Pastor Becker stood up. "You have a lot to think about now. We can set up more counseling if you need to, either individually or as a family unit. Let's pray before we leave."

Page allowed Chase to drive her home. Deep in thought, she hadn't realized that Chase had parked the car. "Mom, are you OK?" Page looked around and refocused on Chase. "I'm sorry. I must have really been lost in thought."

"Anything you want to talk about?"

"No, not right now. I need to work out some things is all. Let's get into the house. The neighbors will wonder what we are doing out here." They gathered their belongings and headed into the house. Page walked to the kitchen to get something to drink. "You want anything while I'm in here?"

"No. Thanks, Mom. I've got some homework, and then I'm headed for bed."

"See you in the morning, honey." Page stood, looking out the window. She thought of Doug and Chase and the possibility of becoming a family. It was almost more than she could imagine. Page shook her head and pushed away from the counter. She needed to clear her head and thought a hot shower would help. There was always work she could dabble in later. Page knew it was going to be a long night of tossing and turning.

Doug headed for home and felt good about how the evening turned out. He hoped that Page would consider a family-type relationship. He knew to take it slow and easy, so she wouldn't be scared off. But he felt it deep in his soul that he needed Page as much as he wanted Chase in his life. In the short time he had been corresponding and now seeing Chase, he loved her more each time they talked. If only he hadn't blown it years ago, he could have had the best of both worlds all this time. Doug decided to contact Chase to set up some type of family outing for the weekend if they would be available. He was anxious to get together as soon as possible. Remembering what Pastor Becker told them, he wouldn't push. Doug smiled. A little nudge in the right direction from Chase would probably be all it took.

Doug contacted Chase and had her work her magic to convince Page to go to the zoo that weekend. Page thought about it and decided that it was a good way to start a family visit and agreed to go. She prayed for guidance during their time together and to give her peace about Doug, so she could enjoy the day. The weekend turned out to be great weather for strolling around the zoo. The three of them roamed all the exhibits and had a great time laughing at the antics of the monkeys and watching birds fly down and swipe their French fries when they were sitting down at lunch. Page found herself enjoying the day tremendously. She looked over at Chase and noticed a look of satisfaction and happiness on her face. "Having fun, Chase?"

"This has been a great day. The weather is awesome, and I have the two best parents there ever was by my side." Page blushed. "I'm sorry, Mom. I didn't think how that might sound to you." Page gave Chase a hug. "It's OK, honey. It's been a great day for me too."

"I second that!" said Doug. They all laughed and headed out the gate toward the car. Doug drove Page and Chase home. "This has been great. I would love to see you two ladies again soon." Page replied, "Come to church tomorrow."

"That's a fine idea. I think we can consider ourselves the topic of conversation with the church ladies for awhile." Page and Chase told Doug they would meet him there at the usual time, and Doug headed for home.

"Mom. You like him don't you?"

"Yes, Chase, I do. He has changed, and the man I see now is even nicer than the man I knew when we first met."

"I'm glad. I love you, Mom, and I have grown to love him too. The missing piece of the puzzle is there. And when I look in the mirror, I see him. Do you know what I mean?"

"Absolutely. When I look at you, I see him too, especially those eyes. I'm so happy you two are getting along so well. I always dreaded the thought of when you would meet him—how everything would go. He explained at our counseling that he wouldn't have been as nice just a couple of years ago. Your dad turned back to God and has repented. He is trying to be a better man now, and all I see is a good man. We will go slow and see if that angry, selfish man shows back up."

"I hope not! I like this one!"

"You skedaddle and get your shower. You smell like the zoo." Chase stuck her tongue out at her mom but headed for the shower.

Chapter 8

Chase was required to fly back to Blue Sky to testify in Mark Petersen's trial. The judge wanted to make sure she had not changed her mind on pressing charges, and he also wanted to see if she had any lingering health issues from her stay on the mountain. Page and Chase prepared to fly out on a Tuesday and planned to stay an extra day to check out the repairs and clean up after the flood. Chase was going to report back to her youth group on the living conditions and whether or not they needed to send further supplies. Chase told her father they were leaving, but she didn't ask him to go with them. Doug thought about offering but held back in case Page had told Chase that she didn't want him to go with them. He finally talked himself into letting it go and didn't say anything. He wished her well and told her to stick to her convictions.

Page picked up a rental car upon arriving at the airport. The drive to Blue Sky was much more pleasant this time, and Chase and Page stopped to take a few pictures along the route. Chase wanted to show her mom the hill the volunteers stopped at when they first headed to Blue Sky and show her where the flooding had been. Chase had told her that was when the group first realized the damage they would be seeing. There was plenty of daylight, and the scenery was beautiful as Page pulled the car over. After they got out and looked at the scene lying before them, Chase realized that the fields were looking much better. They looked across the green pastures to the Blue Sky River, now well between the banks. Chase snapped a few pictures to show her youth group the improvement. The flooded building was still sagging in the mud in the field, but grass was growing and a lot of the debris had been cleaned up. Cattle were grazing quietly through the fields, and Page noticed a few calves off running and jumping. Their antics had both of them laughing so hard it was difficult for Page to settle down to drive on to Blue Sky.

As they pulled up to the motel, Page remembered the last time they were there. She looked over at Chase and smiled. "It's so good to have you home with me again. I can't believe what you went through a few weeks ago, yet you don't seem to have any long-term effects from it. Don't you ever have any nightmares?" Chase thought a moment before answering. She stared out the window, not really seeing the motel in front of her. "You know, Mom, I really don't have any trouble sleeping. I think it's because Mark never set out to hurt me. At first, I was terrified. But as I began to see that he was protecting me, I realized as long as he continued to think I was Becky, I would be just fine. He isn't a bad guy." Chase turned to look at Page. "I think of him a lot. Do you think I could talk to him while we're here? I want him to know I don't hate him. I couldn't stand it if he thought I did. I really can't explain it exactly how I feel, Mom."

"I don't know, Chase. The Sheriff might allow you to see him, but I really don't know. Maybe the judge can help with that."

"Well, I guess we can get some answers tomorrow. Come on, Mom. I'm starved."

"Let's get checked in first, then we can feed you." Page and Chase settled into their room and went across the street for supper. They were both tired after their flight and drive and had no desire to explore Blue Sky any further, so they headed back to their room. They needed to get up early for court, so Page was glad the motel served a light breakfast. Page knew they would both be nervous in the morning and probably wouldn't want a large meal anyway.

The following day, Page drove them over to the court house and found their way to the right court room. It had several pew-like benches on both sides of the aisle, and they chose to sit closer to the front to watch the cases that were scheduled before theirs. They were early enough that they felt more comfortable with their surroundings by the time Mark's lawyer arrived. The Sheriff came over and introduced the Lemons to Mr. Gastron. Chase looked him over and shuddered. Although she shook his hand, she felt that he was formidable and hoped she never had to have someone like that represent her. Mr. Gastron and Page visited briefly before Mark was brought into the courtroom. Mr. Gastron excused himself and walked over to Mark and sat with him at their table. The hearing was going to be held to present the facts only and the judge would make a determination whether Mark would have further charges pressed against him and be held over for a full hearing. Mark had been spending all his time in the local jail since his arrest. There was no bond set as the judge felt that Mark would not return once out.

The hearing began, and Mr. Gastron requested that Mark be reprimanded to his parents' custody and allowed his freedom. No harm had come to Ms. Lemon and none was meant. Mr. Gastron stated that the time Mark had spent in jail would be enough penance for taking Ms. Lemon and holding her briefly. After Mr. Gastron sat down, the judge asked that Chase come forward to talk with him. Chase stood and walked up to the judge. As the judge looked down at Chase, he frowned. "How about you come over to the witness stand and sit down. You look like you're going to fall over you're shaking so badly." Chase worked her way over to the witness stand and took a deep breath and meekly replied. "Thank you, Judge."

"That's fine, Ms. Lemon. Now, why don't we talk a bit about what happened and why you don't want to press charges?"

Chase looked at her mom for support, then turned and looked at Mark. He stared at her with a confused look on his face. "Mark is a nice guy. He treated me respectfully and even made sure I was safe when a bear cub and its momma found us. Mark made sure we ate every day and had plenty to drink. The only thing I want is for him to get some counseling because he needs to face the fact that his sister is gone. I'm not your sister, Mark. My name is Chase, and I'm not mad at you. And I forgive you for taking me against my will. Please get some help, so you can go on with your life." Page turned when she heard noises behind her. There was a man holding his crying wife, and Page thought it was probably Mark's parents. She turned back to Chase. Chase turned to look at the judge. "You see, he was just trying to make up for something with his sister. I don't know what it was, but he isn't a bad person, Judge. He just needs some help." The judge looked down at Chase. "Thank you, Ms. Lemon. You are a very observant young lady. I appreciate you coming all this way to talk to the court. Are you having any health issues of your own related to the stay on the mountain?"

"No, Judge. I'm fine. Really."

"That's fine. Fine. You are dismissed and can go back to your seat. There will be a fifteen minute recess while I take everything under advisement." With that, the judge tapped his gavel and left the room.

Chase returned to her seat, and Page held her shaking daughter. "You did well, Chase."

"At least I got to say something to Mark." They sat there and waited quietly while awaiting the judge's return. Occasionally, Chase would look over at Mark. His lawyer was in a deep conversation with him, and Mark would occasionally turn a concerned face to Chase. When the judge returned and court was in session again, Chase held Page's hand tightly, waiting to hear the future for Mark. The judge looked at Mark and then over to Chase. He asked for Mark to rise, and he and Mr. Gastron did so. "I have taken everything into consideration about this case. It seems to me that Mr. Petersen has been a model prisoner and has caused no further issues while in jail. He is also known to have some aberrant behavior while on Blue Sky Mountain. I am reprimanding Mr. Petersen to a mental health facility until he can accept his sister's demise, and I will expect him to write a letter of apology to Ms. Lemon to be sent through the courts when he has accepted and understood his actions. Until then, he is not to be out of custody for any reason. I agree that with no past record and with the current mental health issue, he has served enough time in jail. Counseling should save this fine man and allow him to become a respectable community member once again. Court dismissed."

As everyone stood as the judge left the courtroom, Chase and Page held each other tightly. Chase looked up at her mom and smiled. "I just hope it doesn't take him too long to figure stuff out, so he can go home again." Just as Page started to respond, she was tapped on the shoulder. "Excuse us, but we want to thank Ms. Lemon for her kind words about our son. We're Mark's parents, and we were so afraid he was going to sit in jail for years. We knew he needed help, but no one would listen to us." Chase reached over and patted Mrs. Petersen on her arm. "It's OK. He'll get help now. I was telling the truth about him treating me just fine. After all, he thought I was his sister." The Sheriff walked over and handed Chase her phone. "Sorry to have kept it so long, but it was evidence. Now that he is going for treatment, we can release it back to you." Chase took the phone and handed it to her mom. "Thank you, Sheriff, but I bought another one to replace it."

"I figured you probably would, but I have to give it back since it's your property."

Page thanked him and turned back to the Petersen family. After visiting with the Petersen's for a short time, they all left the courthouse and went their separate ways.

Chase was ready to head to the mountain and look at it once again. She also wanted to see if people were still living in the cabins and if they needed any supplies. Page drove up to the campground, and they walked closer to the mountain. They stood looking up at the mountain—Chase looking around to find the mine and Page remembering all the hours she spent staring at it waiting for Chase. "Come on, Mom. It's over. Let's go talk to some people." Page looked at Chase and wondered how she had ever raised such a great gal. They spent an hour walking around and talking to several people still living in the cabins. Then, they drove up to the building site; and Chase took some pictures of the finished product. There had been a few additional buildings completed since their group had come and gone, but the shelters in town were empty. Page made a list of supplies needed and texted it to their pastor. Eventually, these shelters would be donated to the park to rent out as cabins. Many of the residents were in the process of rebuilding and repairing their own homes. Some stated they didn't have any insurance and would be waiting for an apartment to open up before being able to move out of the cabins. Others said they would be moving away from Blue Sky closer to other family members as not only their homes but also their jobs were gone. The flood had devastated many families and their normal day-to-day lives.

After returning to their motel after supper, Page and Chase reviewed the day's events and felt they had accomplished everything they set out to do while in Blue Sky. They were ready to return home tomorrow. As they turned off the lights that evening, Chase prayed for Mark to get well soon. The following day remained uneventful as they returned home. The stress of the previous day remained, and they were both glad to be home once again. Doug called Chase that evening to check on their trip, but Chase yawned through most of the conversation. Doug told her he would check on her the next evening and that he was glad everything had gone well while Page and Chase were in Blue Sky. Doug still wished he had gone with them. The problem, he decided, was that he wanted to do everything with them. He was becoming very impatient again. "I'm such a hurry-up kind of guy." Doug shook his head and decided to get his own shower and get ready for bed.

Doug called Page the following day and offered to take them out for supper that evening. He explained that they would be too tired to cook at home; and after their trip, they deserved a night out to relax. Page agreed, and they set up a time for Doug to stop by to pick them up. Page hung up and looked out the window. "What are you doing?" She shook her head and went back to work. That evening, they were both ready when Doug arrived. "Dad, sorry I was so tired last night. I probably didn't make any sense." Doug smiled. We can talk about it tonight if you want. Or we can talk about anything *but* that. The choice is yours. I knew you would be starving either way." Chase reached over and punched Doug on the arm. Doug took them out for pizza, and they had a good time listening to Chase talk about antics of her classmates at school. Page hadn't heard all of the recent stories, so she was as entertained as Doug. Chase was talking about finding a job that summer as an older couple passed by their table. The woman stopped and told them that it was good to see a family enjoying themselves so much. They all looked at each other, and Page mumbled a thank you. After the couple left, Page replied, "That was nice but uncomfortable." Doug looked over at her. "Well, we *are* having fun!" At that, they all laughed once again. Page had to agree that they were having fun—and as a family.

Doug dropped everyone off at home that evening and set up a time to see Chase that weekend. Chase was excited about school being out for another year, and he wanted to spend as much time as he could with her while he had the chance. She was growing up so fast, and he had missed out on so much of her life. He knew he could never make it up to her but hoped he could always be in her life from now on.

When Chase finished classes for the year, she visited with her mom about several job opportunities and was having a difficult time deciding on what she should do for the summer. "Chase, have you settled on a career yet? That would help you decide on your summer job."

"After my encounter with Mark this last year, I think I want to look at psychology, counseling, or something along those lines. I realized there is so much need in that area, but I don't know what I could do as far as a summer job." Page thought about this revelation, and in terms of Chase's long-term commitment to help people like Mark. "I think that's a commendable line of work, and you are a very compassionate young lady. How about you look into volunteering for summer camps? They have some in the area that are for disabled kids, troubled kids, and maybe we can look into some other camps. I'm sure that the church camps could use some help too. You're lucky enough that you don't really need to get a paid position, but some of those will offer something for your time." "That's a great idea, Mom. I hadn't thought about camps! And you know how much I love being outside! I'm going to go look some up right now and see what's available" Chase rushed off to her room to get on the computer. Page smiled. Her little girl was growing up way too fast.

Chase found several camps and applied for positions at five of them. She was approved for three and was excited to be able help out and enjoy being outside for the summer. Page was helping her pack for the first camp, and Chase talked nonstop about all the things she was going to get to do and the types of kids she would be able to help. In addition, she still had a few free weeks that she could go to her own church youth camp and have fun with kids her own age. Page thought back to her own childhood and how much she had missed out on because of her need to work instead of enjoying her summers doing things like Chase. She wouldn't trade her life for anything and knew that what she learned as a child would always be with her. It made her the woman she was today, faults and all, but it also helped her raise Chase in a different type of environment. All in all, she was quietly pleased with the way Chase turned out, despite having been a single parent and one that was raised by uninvolved parents of her own. Sure, they had their problems along the way, but Chase was raised with respect and responded to others with respect as well.

Doug took Chase out for a walk at the local park before she left on her first camp trip. They talked about menial things but also what Chase expected to learn through her summer experiences. Doug hoped to continue to find time with Chase off and on as the summer went on but knew a summer vacation was going to be out of the question with all of her activities. She was going to be busy and Doug was beginning to miss her already. "Dad, while I'm gone, call up Mom and take her out instead of me. She's going to need the company since I'm going to be gone so much."

"Hmmm. That sounds like a great idea. And we can have a chance to talk about you while you're gone." Chase slapped Doug on the arm playfully. "Hey! Don't be ganging up on me! I won't be here to defend myself!" Doug gave her a little shove back. "It was your idea, ya' know!" They continued to walk several laps around the park and stopped to feed the koi fish. When Doug took Chase home, he walked in the house with her and approached Page. "Chase leaves on

Sunday after church. How about we go to lunch and a movie? It will take your mind off our little one going off to do grownup things." Page laughed and agreed it sounded like a great idea. Chase smiled at them both and went to her room. Doug and Page talked about their individual projects at work over a glass of iced tea before Doug excused himself to head for home. "I'll see you in a few days"

"Looking forward to it. See you at church."

As soon as Chase drove off for her first camp of the summer, Doug took Page to grab a sandwich before heading over to the movie theater. They talked about work and their daughter. Page noticed she was comfortable around Doug once again. It was almost as if the last several years hadn't happened, and they were once again good friends. They went to the theater and discussed the options for movies before agreeing on one. The line was short since it was early in the day, so purchasing popcorn and a drink didn't take very long. Their movie wouldn't be starting for a few minutes, and they had a chance to play a few arcade games while they waited. Doug and Page couldn't believe how bad they both were and laughed heartily over their attempts to beat each other. Before long, it was time for them to get to their seats. As they sat down and ensconced their drinks safely in the holders, Doug turned and looked at Page and smiled. He reached over and picked up her hand. Page looked down and then at Doug. She smiled and gave his hand a quick hug just as the lights lowered. He would let go of her hand only long enough to handle his drink or eat popcorn but would soon pick it up again. Page could hardly concentrate on the movie. She felt as giddy as a girl on her first date.

Once the movie was over, Doug and Page picked up their trash and dumped it on the way out of the theater. As they walked out of the building, Doug reached over and took Page's hand once again. They were quiet as they walked to the car. He led her to her door and opened it, allowing her to get in before quietly closing it for her. Doug jumped in the driver's seat and turned to look at Page. "I just want you to know that this has been the best day out I've had in seventeen years."

"I agree, Doug. It has been wonderful. Thank you so much." Doug turned and started the car. "If you're not ready to go home yet, how about I take you for a drive out around the lake and then grab a bite to eat?"

"That sounds good. I'm not ready to end the day either." Doug smiled and turned the car for the short drive toward the lake. Two hours later, they two of them parked at an Italian restaurant. "It's been a wonderful day, Page. I hope to spend more time with you just like this in the near future." Page agreed completely that the day was terrific and was anxious to spend more time with Doug. "Me too, but in Chase's words, I'm starved." They laughed and Doug jumped out of the car to open her door and then led her into the restaurant to complete their evening.

As the summer wore on, Page and Doug spent more and more time together. When Chase was home, they got together for family outings and Chase always had plenty of adventures to talk to them about. Toward the end of the summer, Chase had a few weeks home before her last year of school started. She suddenly realized the changes that had taken place in her parent's relationship with each other. She arranged a day of school shopping with her mom; and as they had stopped for a bite to eat, Chase looked over at her mom with a questioning look. Page noticed and sent a look back. "What?"

"I'm waiting to hear all about you and Dad." Page looked at her and took a moment to decide what to say. She looked away and watched the mall traffic for a bit. "Your dad and I have been seeing each other quite a bit. You know it's your fault anyway when you told him to take me out since you would be gone." Page turned to look at Chase and saw she was grinning from ear to ear. Page turned a shade of pink Chase had never seen. "Mom. I can't believe you're embarrassed! You have feelings for him, don't you?"

"It's hard to explain, Chase. Years ago, I was so devastated by his leaving me, especially knowing I was pregnant with you. So I just put him out of my mind all those years and gave him so little thought. But once the tornado hit Smith Falls and then you were kidnapped, Doug being in my life has never seemed so right. I realized sometime this summer that I never did quit loving him. I just put it on hold. That's why no one else seemed interesting to me all these years. No one could ever come close to the man I knew your dad to be. What we went through as a young couple could have been salvaged if we both hadn't been so proud and stubborn. It was stupid for us both, and you and your dad missed out on a lot of years."

"Mom, I know it was hard for you, but I don't blame either one of you. We all make stupid mistakes. And Dad is wonderful. I know you both blame yourselves, but I'm good. Really. But I would like to see the two of you get back together and make us a complete family once again." Page turned a thoughtful face to the crowds again. "We'll see, Chase. It's been a lot for your Dad and I to work through, but the relationship has grown. And we do enjoy spending time as a family." They gathered up their bags and left to finish up their shopping, both thinking about Doug in their own way.

Doug spent some time doing some shopping of his own. He was speculating on Page and Chase agreeing to a long weekend adventure with him to a place of Chases' choice. They had been having a great time as a family unit, and he wanted to make sure it continued. Chase would be busy in her last year of high school, then she would be off to college. There wouldn't be much more time he could spend in the next few months taking them anywhere. He stopped by a travel agency and picked out a few brochures to give to Chase. As he left to drive over to their house, he smiled and set some plans of his own into motion. Chase was excited to be able to choose her own destination. Page thought he was spoiling her too much but knew he was just trying to make up time with her. Chase narrowed it down to two choices, and they all discussed the pros and cons of the trip and how much time they would need to enjoy it sufficiently. After deciding on a trip to the Grand Canyon and agreeing to take the long mule ride down into the canyon, they got a calendar, looked at their own busy work schedule, and picked a date that would work for all of them. Since they picked Labor Day weekend to fit everyone's schedule, Page and Chase got out the computer and reserved motel rooms and cabins and their trip down the canyon. Once that was completed, Doug made flights and car reservations. They were all getting excited to go on a family vacation and talked about all the things they would be able to do while there. The girls decided they had to go on another shopping trip to buy boots and floppy hats. Doug just laughed and told them he would see them later and that he would leave them to their shopping details. Doug left and arranged a few other details of the trip and then realized he needed to pick up a few clothing items for the trip too, but he wasn't going to tell the girls!

A couple of weeks later found them getting off a plane in Flagstaff, Arizona, and picking up the rental car for the drive North. They had a great flight and were excited to finally land and to be headed for their destination. They stopped for their first night in Tusayan and checked into their rooms. Since they had decided to do this trip spur of the moment, all the rooms at the Grand Canyon Lodge were full. The girls excitedly unpacked a few items and talked about their trip. Doug said he would wait for them out by the car, and they could decide where to eat after they met up. During supper, they talked about how they would be site seeing the North rim before taking their ride down into the canyon. The motel rooms were reserved for their whole trip, so they could leave the majority of their travel items behind and just take their back packs with them and not have to leave behind any personal items in the car. They all agreed to take only what the brochure told them to make sure they had, and nothing else. It was going to be a long trek and no one wanted to carry anything too heavy for a couple of days. Chase said she would make sure to take a lot of pictures for everyone and reminded Page that she could carry the extra batteries in her pack.

The next day, they drove into the park and casually followed the road to areas that had pull offs for outstanding views or educational findings. One of the places they all enjoyed was the museum on the Indians that had once lived in the area. They took the hike around the areas that once housed them and read the educational plaques. There was a park ranger available for questions and Chase took a lot of pictures of the site. It was amazing to see how the Indians had once lived, attempting to grow food on a plateau so far from water. They ended the day at the large visitor center and a great view of the canyon. Doug left the girls to check on their scheduled trek to make sure they were still on tap for the mule ride as planned. Doug brought back the details of time and place for arrival. They all talked about it excitedly on their way back to the car. They drove back to the motel, cleaned up, and met for supper; they decided what time they would need to be ready to go the following morning. Since it would have to be early because they had a bit of drive time, they picked up a few breakfast-to-go items. Doug bought a few extra granola bars to throw in their packs too. "I'll see you girls bright and early in the morning! Don't be late!" The girls waved at him, and they each went to their rooms to settle in for the night. They were all exhausted from the long, hot day, and Page hoped they would sleep well since the next day would be longer and more arduous than today. Page packed her backpack while Chase showered. She remembered the batteries and set her floppy hat on top of her boots. Chase came out of the shower and saw the backpack. "I forgot I hadn't packed yet. Don't let me forget my camera!" Page took her shower and, when she was ready for bed, checked both their backpacks for missing items. "I think we have everything. Hopefully Doug and his granola bars will hold out!" They both chuckled and settled into bed for the night. Page could hear Chase toss and turn but finally heard her quiet relaxed breathing, telling her she finally went to sleep. Page turned one more time and punched her pillow. She was so worried about Chase not sleeping she hadn't realized she was wide awake. She thought over the trip so far and how much she was enjoying the time together. She smiled and gradually dropped off to sleep thinking of Doug.

The following morning, they hurried to the car as they were excited to get to the Grand Canyon once again. Doug drove to the Bright Angel Lodge and managed to have a few minutes to spare by the time they parked and gathered their belongings. As a handful of other riders gathered, they circled around their wrangler as he provided information on their trip. The wranglers then individually saddled the riders on their mounts and made sure everything was ready for their trip. The decent would be ten and a half miles and would take them several hours. The ride included lunch, and a beautiful ride was guaranteed while crossing the rock face of Inner Gorge, the Suspension Bridge, and then up to the Phantom Ranch where they would spend the evening in furnished cabins. The ride impressed everyone, the wrangler was educational and had a few old jokes that made you laugh because they were so bad; and by the time they reached the ranch, everyone was stiff and sore. The wranglers helped everyone get off the mules and told them all to walk and stretch for a while before attempting to sit once again. The view was gorgeous, and the three walked around the area quietly with Chase continuing to take pictures of everything and everyone. Once they felt loosened up again, they found their cabins and dropped their backpacks on the bed. Supper would be ready in an hour or two, so they had time to relax and clean up. Chase beat Page to the shower; so Page went outside and sat on the porch, waiting for Chase to finish up. She was enjoying the surroundings and had almost fallen asleep when Chase came outside and startled her. "It's all yours, Mom!" Page jumped up and looked around. "I can't believe I went to sleep." Chase chuckled. "I wasn't in the shower that long!"

"I must either be really tired from the ride or just relaxed."

"Probably a combination of both, Mom. Go get your shower, or we'll be late for supper." "I know, I know. You're starved!" Chase stuck her tongue out at her mom as Page turned and went in to clean up. Chase sat down and looked at the surroundings. As she began to relax, she realized exactly why her mom had dozed off. It was beautiful and quiet.

Page took her shower and put on fresh clothes. She tidied up the bathroom and arranged their clothes for the next day. Chase had already used up a couple of batteries, and she could see that she had changed out two more. Page shook her head. "Chase must have taken a thousand pictures by now." She joined Chase on the porch until they heard the dinner bell ring. As they walked toward the dining hall, they were joined by Doug. He was yawning as he came along side of them. "I don't think I'm going to have any problem sleeping tonight." Doug yawned again followed by Chase and Page. "Stop yawning, Dad. You'll have us all asleep in our food!" Doug shook his head and put an arm around both of their shoulders and walked them to the dining hall. As they sat down, he stayed between the two and kept a leg in contact with Page through the whole meal. When he finished, he put his arm on the back of the chairs and said he was ready for a little walk before bed to settle his food. The girls agreed and after thanking the cook, they wandered off and watched the night settle in. As it became cooler, the girls decided they needed to return to the cabin. "Page, could you stay here for a moment? I want to talk to you a bit."

"I guess. You OK with going to the cabin by yourself, Chase? I'll be right there."

"Sure, Mom. You two enjoy yourselves. I'm getting ready for bed." Chase casually headed for the cabin and, once at the door, turned and waved at Doug and Page. They waved back before turning to the canyon in front of them. Doug reached over and tugged on Page's hand. "Walk with me a bit." As they walked a short distance, Doug found a boulder and lifted Page up to sit on it. Looking up at Page, he started to say something when four of their group walked up and began visiting about their ride. It was becoming much cooler and Page had become uncomfortable, so she excused herself to go back to the cabin and left Doug with the others. When Page opened the cabin, she noticed Chase was sound asleep. She was ready to join her and got ready quickly. As she jumped under the covers, she was surprised at how comfortable the bed was. She stretched out and took a few deep breaths. The next thing she knew it was morning.

After a hearty breakfast, everyone mounted up for the ride back. This trip back was almost two miles shorter as they would be returning on the South Kaibab Trail. At the rim, they would be taken back to the Bright Angel Lodge by a driver. The trip back was just as successful and Chase continued to take picture after picture. During the trip down and back, the wranglers would stop and discuss geologic formations, ecology, past human history, and many other interesting items. They answered questions from the group easily and always treated them with respect. The whole group enjoyed their wrangler and agreed it would be fun to take another trip. As the three made their way back to their car, they were joined by others from the group; and they all said their good-byes as they opened the car door. Doug started the car and waited for the air conditioning to kick in. As the coolness began blowing, he closed the door and buckled up. "I'm ready to head back to the motel unless you two wanted to do something else before we leave." Chase leaned over the seat. "We have to go to the gift shop and get something from the trip besides blisters!" Doug and Page both laughed so hard they had tears in their eyes. I'll drive up closer and leave the car running while you two go in. I'm done moving for a while and want to sit in the air conditioning." Doug let them out at the door and drove around the parking lot to find a spot where he could see them come back out. After parking, he laid his head back and thought about the trip. He almost dropped off to sleep when he heard a car door slam next to him. Just as he looked back to the gift shop, he saw the girls come out laughing with their arms piled high with bags. Doug groaned and put the car in gear. As he pulled up next to them, he popped the trunk for their packages. Once they were tucked away and the girls got into the car and seat belts on, he put the car in gear and headed back to the motel. Once they got back and unloaded, they all agreed to a light supper and an early night. They had to catch a plane the next day and everyone wanted to be well rested for the trip home. Page and Chase had to figure out how to pack all the extras so it would fit into their luggage, so they spent the next hour taking care of the packing before meeting Doug for supper.

After a great night's sleep, everyone was ready to head for home. They caught their plane and managed to make it home without incident. As Doug helped the girls unload their luggage, he asked them if they wanted to go get a bite to eat. Page yawned and said she was ready to call it a day. Chase concurred, so Doug left them and returned to his apartment. He mulled over the trip. Not everything went as planned, so he would have to come up with Plan B. He pulled his luggage into his apartment. As he flopped on the sofa, he didn't blame the girls for calling it a night. He was exhausted and decided he would make it an early night too.

Chapter 9

Everyone went back to their own lives once they returned from the Grand Canyon. Chase started her senior year in high school and was going to be very busy with not only her homework but all the extracurricular activities she had signed up for. She was also highly involved in her youth group at church and would help lead the younger teens during projects. Page had a new client that involved an extremely large project out of state and found it was going to have her traveling quite a bit as they put the early pieces together. Doug had hit the road as soon as he returned to work. He was needed back in his old office for a while, developing a project for one of his previous clients that had mandated he either help him or he would find someone else. Doug knew that the temperamental client wasn't kidding and was happy to smooth some ruffled feather as it would have lost the company significant revenue if they lost the account. Doug had wooed the gentleman several years back, and they had hit off personally. Doug felt that he was just lonely and needed to see his friend once again and wasn't really mad at anyone in the office.

Doug called Chase frequently in the late evenings to catch her before bed. It was the best time for them both due to their busy schedules. He frequently asked Chase how her mom was doing; and finally, Chase told him to call her himself. He thought about it for a few days before doing so. Page had been back and forth, seeing to her project and worked in her home office at night once Chase was home and busy with her own homework. She could hear Chase talk to her father occasionally, and wistfulness would come over her. She hadn't seen nor heard from Doug for three weeks, two days, and fourteen hours; but she wasn't counting. Late that evening, her own phone rang. When she saw it was Doug, her stomach flipped over.

Page answered. "Hello, stranger. How are you?"

"I'm fine but tired of all this running around. I'll be home and done with traveling by the weekend. How about yourself?"

"I have one more trip this week and next, then I think I will be done for a while. It's been pretty hectic, working on this project. I may even send someone else next week, depending on how it looks from this end."

"Sounds good. I'll check with Chase, but do you know if she'll be home this weekend?"

"I think so. We talked about it briefly at supper, and she thought she had the weekend free. Why?"

"I just thought I'd come over since it has been so long."

"Sure. Come on by. I think we will just be *vegging*." Doug chuckled. Maybe I will come by and "veg" with you! I'll call you guys Saturday morning."

"Sounds good. And, Doug?"

"Yea?"

"It was good to talk to you."

"You too, Page. See you Saturday."

The week flew by, and the thought of seeing Doug on the weekend kept Page's nervous energy flowing. She finished up several loose ends on a few projects and arranged to have a junior partner fly out next week to check on things at their latest project. Doug planned to arrive around eleven, Saturday morning; and they would plan something after his arrival. Page and Chase were lounging in the living room when he arrived. Chase bounced up and answered the door and brought him to the living room. He looked around and the magazines and books scattered around their seating areas. "You weren't kidding when you said you would be *vegging*." They all laughed and invited him to sit and "veg."

"Sounds good. Then we'll go find a place for lunch. How about Chinese" They agreed that sounded good and the proceeded to return to their own magazines and books. About 12:30 p.m., Chase's stomach growled so loudly they all heard it. Doug looked over at her and said, "I guess the dinner bell rang!" They all jumped up and headed out the door. Doug took them to the local Chinese buffet; and once they got their food and were chowing down, Doug asked Chase what she was going to be doing the following weekend. "Well, let's see." She grabbed out her phone and looked at the calendar. "I have a game out of town Friday night and practice on Saturday. Saturday night I have something at church for a couple of hours. Sunday is church, of course. Somewhere in that time, I have some homework to do." Doug looked over at Page. "What are *you* doing this next weekend?"

"Nothing. Absolutely, gloriously, nothing." Doug thought about it for a bit. "How about you take me to Smith Falls and show me around. You can show me that new hospital you developed and where you grew up. What do you think?"

"Hmm. I suppose that would work. But we would need to go down on Friday night and come back Saturday night. I want to be home for Chase and then church on Sunday."

"Great. You make a motel reservation wherever you like to stay, and I'll meet you over here on Friday after work. Deal?"

"Deal. And I should take you out to the falls. That is how the town got its name, you know. The falls are beautiful. And this time of year, the trees are turning. And it will be gorgeous."

"Great!" They finished with their meal and returned to Page's house. Chase left them talking in the living room and said she had homework to do. She smiled like a Cheshire cat as she left the two together.

Doug left work late in the day and headed for home. He had some laundry to throw in, and he needed a few groceries—having been gone so much he had little in the way of sustenance. As he puttered around, he thought of Page and their trip. He had planned on talking to her at the Grand Canyon and just as he started, he was interrupted by other riders. Then Page left for her cabin and he didn't have another chance. He thought this would be a perfect time as it would be the two of them, and there should be no interruptions. He finished his errands and settled in for the night. His apartment seemed so cold and empty even though Chase had helped him decorate. It only came alive when she was there.

The week flew by for everyone. Page said good-bye to Chase on their way out the door and reminded her that she would she wouldn't be there when she got home late that night, that she was headed to Smith Falls. Chase smiled and said she remembered quite well and to have a good time. After work, Page threw a few items together for the trip in her overnight bag. She was a light traveler; and having been on the road frequently, she knew what a necessity was and what wasn't. She was ready and waiting when Doug arrived. They transferred his bag into her car and hit the road. It was a pleasant fall drive, and the leaves were beginning to change. Page pointed out a variety of things along the route, and the trip seemed to fly by. Doug was never in sports in school, nor had he traveled much during that time. And he never even thought of driving toward Smith Falls in all the years he lived in the area, so it was a pleasant surprise to see the attractions along the way.

When they pulled up to the motel, Doug insisted he pay for it since it was his idea. Page argued that he had taken care of the Grand Canyon trip, and she could well afford a motel for one night. He finally agreed but insisted he pay for supper. "I'll meet you by the car in a few minutes, Doug. I'm starved."

"Now I know where Chase gets the appetite from!" Page opened up her room and stuck her tongue out at him. "I'm only starving because you're paying!" Then, she ducked into the room and left him standing there, unable to get in the last word. Page met him ten minutes later and drove them to a nice family style restaurant; and as they perused the menu, Doug would ask about different meals. They were finally ready to order and while waiting for their meal, they people watched. Page would point out different individuals she knew and what they did. "I don't really know anyone anymore, but I still know some faces." About that time, Ms. Yancy arrived with several of her friends. Page stood up and waved at her. Ms. Yancy walked over and took a long look at Doug as she hugged Page. "Who is this fine specimen of a man?" Doug stood up and introduced himself. Ms. Yancy shook his hand. "You must be Chase's father. She looks just like you."

"Yes, Madame. That I am."

"Well, I'm Ms. Yancy, and don't you be hurting my girl anymore. You understand? Or you will have to deal with me!" Ms. Yancy stood with her hands on her hips, giving him a ferocious scowl. Page thought she better run interference and rushed to talk to her. "Ms. Yancy. It's so good to see you again. I was going to call you tomorrow, but now that we have the introductions out of the way, that won't be necessary. I'm showing Doug around Smith Falls tomorrow. Chase was busy this weekend, so we got a couple of rooms at the motel tonight and will head out tomorrow afternoon sometime." About that time, their meal arrived; and Ms. Yancy grabbed Page in a big hug. "You take care and keep in touch with me more often. I need to know how this came all about. I never could get you to talk about yourself." She released Page and turned to look at Doug and shook her finger at him. "I mean it!" Then, she turned and stalked over to her own table and proceeded to tell them all about the visit she just had.

"That's quite a friend you have there. I can't remember who you told me she was?" Page proceeded to remind Doug of how Ms. Yancy came into her life and also about Grace. "I want to stop at the cemetery tomorrow too, if that's all right with you." "That's fine. Wherever or whatever you want to show me. We'll save Smith Falls for last as it's on our way out of town. They finished up their meals, and Page drove them by her old street and downtown. She talked about the tornado and what Chase and Page did to help out afterwards. They returned to the motel and got out of the car. Doug reached out to take Page's hand. He leaned over and gave her a kiss on the cheek. "Thanks for bringing me here." Page blushed. "No, thank you for having me bring you. It's good to just come and look at things without the drama or work-related things to do with." They talked for a few moments before heading to their rooms. "Meet me at the car about eight. We'll go have a nice breakfast before we head out about town."

"Sounds good." Doug walked over to Page and gave her a gentle kiss on the lips, pulled back, and smiled. "Sounds real good." He left her standing there, this time gaping at him as he opened his door and closed it behind him. It took her a few seconds before she dreamily unlocked her own door and went in.

After breakfast, they headed over to the hospital for their first stop. They sat in the parking lot as she described how it had been built in sections to provide care as quickly as possible. The clinic was completed later, and it was fully functional at this time. Page was proud of the green energy facility she helped create and knew it would last for years, barring another tornado. They then went in for a quick tour, quietly walking the halls as she pointed out different areas. The gardens out front and back offered quiet solace for staff and patients alike and even though it was fall and most of the flowers were long gone, it was still vibrant with fall plants and tree leaves. It was still warm enough that the small waterfalls simulating Smith Falls were still running.

They left their tour of the hospital and drove around town, showing the schools, neighborhoods, churches, and pointing out the areas that were devastated by the tornado and how far the town had come rebuilding since then. They grabbed a late lunch at a sandwich shop and drove to the cemetery. Page led Doug to her parent's grave first. After a few moments, she then led him to Grace's. Doug allowed Page all the quiet time she needed before moving on. Page adjusted the flowers on both graves and mumbled a few words to each. Doug stood back and watched Page deal with the deaths of her loved ones. He thought to himself how long it had been since he had been out to his own mother's gravesite and felt a bit embarrassed. He hadn't even taken out flowers since the funeral. Page led Doug back to the car quietly and then pulled out and headed for Smith Falls. Page sighed. "It always brings me a type of peace to come here. I can't explain it, but ever since I faced my past, it has been a lot easier to deal with all their deaths." Doug just nodded and thought about how he felt about his own mother. He watched the scenery and finally said, "You know, I think you taught me something in this trip. I better go see my mom's cemetery and take some flowers out there. I don't think I've given it enough thought over the years."

"It's tough to face it, but once you do, there is certain peace." Doug nodded again.

As they pulled into the parking lot by the falls, they noticed a few other cars in the lot. "The Falls attract a lot of people. There are hiking trails around, and then, there is the boardwalk to the Falls. There is a bench or two up at the falls if I remember it right. You can sit and just watch them as long as you want. It's great. I haven't been up here in years, so things might have changed. But with the amount of cars here, probably not. And since it is getting later in the day, many of them have probably been here a long time and will be headed out. You better get a jacket because it will be a lot cooler by the time we get up to the falls. The water really chills the surroundings." Page popped the trunk, and they both dug out a jacket. Doug fumbled about his bag a little more and finally shut the trunk. They began their ascent on the boardwalk and met several people coming back down. It was a pleasant hike with several stops along the way to see the river flowing. Page stopped Doug once and pointed out deer in the trees, that were looking back at them. They watched for a time before the deer bounded off away from the area. As they reached the top, they found they had it to themselves. They sat on a bench and Doug reached over for her hand. He sat there watching the falls, slowing rubbing his thumb in a circular motion. "This is really nice. I'm glad you brought me here." Page nodded and continued to watch the falls. She was happy and content, sitting here, having her hand held by Doug. She didn't want the feeling to stop.

After about a half an hour, Doug decided he better talk to Page before she was ready to leave or someone showed up. Just as he said her name, another couple showed up and sat on an adjoining bench. They were talking loudly and not even paying attention to the falls. Doug realized that the couple evidently had been drinking as they were becoming more obnoxious in the short time they had arrived. When they pulled a drink out of their backpack, Doug knew they would have to leave. He took Page's hand and tugged her up. He mouthed, "Let's go." The other couple yelled at them to stay and have a good time, but Page and Doug ignored them and headed back down the boardwalk. As they got out of earshot, Page sighed.

"Nothing like ruining a quiet time." Doug nodded and wondered if he would ever get to talk to Page. As they reached the car, Doug pulled Page over to him. He leaned back on the hood of the car and pulled her to him. "Page, I keep getting interrupted when I want to talk to you. I guess there isn't going to be any perfect setting, but I have got to talk to you." Just then, another car pulled up. "Page, take me to a quiet spot where we won't be interrupted." They got into the car and Page nervously thought about where to go. She headed out of town toward Johnstown and pulled off at a monument marker a few miles down the road. "People don't tend to stop here, so this should work. But we'll stay in the car just in case." Doug nodded and reached over to take Page's hand, licked his lips, and swallowed hard.

"Page, we've lost a lot of years together. I regret it completely. Not having you and Chase in my life was inexcusable, and we will never get that time back. I was such a jerk to you, but I could have been a man about the whole thing. Look, Chase loves us both. I love you, and I know you love me. Would you make me the happiest man on earth and become my wife and a father to Chase?" Page was completely thrown off. She expected him to ask to date her or something similar, but not a marriage proposal. "I don't know what to say. You surprised me!" Doug reached into his jacket pocket and opened a ring case. As he extended it to her, he said, "Please, Page? Make me a happy man." Page reached over to the ring and brought it closer to her. Doug took it out of the box and put it on her finger. "Say yes, Page." Doug looked at their shaking hands. "We're like teenagers on our first date. We're both so nervous." Page looked over at Doug, then down at the ring, then back to Doug. "I love you, Doug. I always have. And I'd be happy to finally call us a family." Doug took Page in his arms and kissed her sweetly on the lips and then held her close. A car honked as they passed. Doug and Page laughed and released each other. "Let's go home and talk to Chase, Page. I'm sure she will approve. I think she's been pushing us together for a long time, the sneaky little girl that she is." Page had to agree; and as she pulled back onto the highway, they both were smiling. And Doug hung onto her hand off and on during the trip home.

As they pulled into the driveway at Page's house, they noticed that Chase was home. Page turned to Doug. "You ready for the screaming teenager routine?"

"Ready as I'll ever be. Let's go!" Page popped the trunk, so Doug could get his overnight bag out and put it in his car. Page let herself into the house with her own bag and told Doug to come in whenever he was ready. Page took her bag toward her room and called out to Chase as she went through the house. Chase yelled back she would be right out. she was getting dressed after a shower. Doug let himself in and waited for them both in the living room. Chase came out first and they caught up on Chase's game results and what she had been up to. Doug had just started to tell her about their trip to Smith Falls when Page came into the room. "Anyone want something to drink?" No one needed anything, so Page let herself down into her favorite recliner. She curled up and watched the interchange between the two as Doug talked about seeing Smith Falls from her mother's eyes. He even talked about having to leave Smith Falls because of the inebriated couple being so obnoxious and loud. "Then, we left town to head for home, and your mom pulled off at a monument marker. And I asked her to marry me." He paused. It took Chase a few seconds for the remark to register. *"You did what? Are you kidding me! Did she say yes?"*

Doug and Page cringed at the screaming. Page reached her hand toward Chase and showed her the ring. Chase jumped on top of Page and hugged her and kept yelling about how awesome it was they were going to be a family. Then, she jumped up and ran over to Doug and tackled him on the couch and did the same thing. As she calmed down, Doug looked over at Page. "I think she approves."

They all laughed at his remark. Chase wasn't done yet. She fired off several questions in a row. "When are you getting married? Where are you getting married? Where are we going to live? Can I be the maid of honor? Who is going to be your best man?" Doug grabbed her and pulled her down. "*Whoa*, Missy! We haven't talked about any of that yet. We needed your approval first. You can help us with all of those decisions as this affects us as a family."

"I'm just so excited this is finally happening! I gotta go call Jenny and tell her!" Chase ran from the room. Page looked over to Doug. "They've been best friends since grade school. I'm not surprised she would want to call her."

"Well, Chase did have some legitimate questions. But I'm tired from the trip. How about we go out to dinner after church and have some of those discussions?"

"Sounds good. It will give time for Chase to list out everything she wants to cover." They both got up and Page walked Doug to the door, where he held her close, kissed her lovingly, and said good night. Page watched Doug walk to the car and waved as he drove off. She thought about the night she watched him drive off about eighteen years ago. "No comparison." She smiled as she listened to Chase talk excitedly to her friend about her parents becoming engaged. It was time to come full circle.

Epilogue

As the holidays rolled around, Chase received a letter from the Blue Sky courts. She and her mom sat down at the kitchen table, and Chase nervously opened it up. Before pulling out the contents, Chase looked at her mom and said, "You know, I've been praying for Mark. This must mean he's better now."

"Let's hope so, Chase. I know that all you wanted was for him to stop being delusional. With that letter, it must be so." The first letter was from the courts explaining that Mark was released to his parents just before Thanksgiving and was on probation. He must continue outpatient therapy for an additional ninety days or until his therapist believed he was no longer in danger to himself and others. In addition, he must provide proof of work hours by the first of the year to show he was able to care for himself. As a final condition, Mark had to write a letter of apology, which was enclosed. Mark was not to try to contact her at any time in the future, and she was to contact the courts if he tried. If she had any further questions, she could contact the judge or sheriff at any time. Chase looked over at her mom and handed her the letter. "That's pretty straight forward." Page took the letter as Chase looked at the letter from Mark.

Dear Ms. Lemon,

I apologize for taking you against your will. I still can't believe I would do such a thing, but a mixed up mind evidently makes you do things you wouldn't normally do. I appreciate you not pressing charges and asking the courts to get me help. Sitting in the jail cell was making me more confused every day. And when I saw you in court, I couldn't figure out what you were telling me. I left the courts and was taken to a facility where I received daily counseling and some medications. My parents started to come to a family counseling session every week, and they realized they were still mourning in their own way and unable to cope. Being sent away was the best thing for all of us, as we all have worked through a lot of family issues and it has brought us all closer together.

I'm now living with my parents and working for my dad. He is trying to get his business back on its feet again. And even though I'm not getting paid yet, it has been good for us both to have a goal for the future.

I'm off all my medication but the antidepressant. My parents are also on it, but as we finish up counseling, the doctor has been cutting our doses back a little at a time. And we hope to be off of everything in a few months.

I want to especially thank you for the kindness you showed me not only in the courts, but while I held you captive. You evidently understood my illness without understanding the details. I would look at you, and my mind tried to tell me you weren't Becky. But I just couldn't let that detail come through. I noticed you praying several times and how it calmed you when you were upset. I couldn't figure out how to ask you about that as we never prayed as a family. In the hospital, I was expected to attend chapel on Sunday. Once the medications became effective, the pastor made more sense to me. I asked my parents to attend with me one Sunday. And afterward, we decided to find a church close to home. We aren't what you call saved yet, but we are at a better understanding of its meaning.

Thank you so much for your patience, and God Bless You and your family. I'll be forever in your debt.

Sincerely,
Mark Petersen

Chase looked up at her mom with tears in her eyes. "This is just wonderful, Mom. Here. Read this." Page took the letter and read it thoroughly. As she handed it back to Chase, she smiled. "You did good honey. You did real good. I would have prosecuted him for what he did to you, but you knew that all he needed was a little help. I'm so proud of you!" They reached out and held each other's hands for a bit. Chase began to pray for Mark and his parents to continue to find peace that only he could bring and to help them continue on the road to recovery. Page added a solemn *amen.* Chase gathered up her papers and said she would show her dad when he came for supper that evening.

The holidays flew by and wedding plans were all Chase and Page could talk about. Although it was going to be held in their church and the plan was for it to be attended by a limited amount of people, they decided to have a Sunday afternoon banquet for the members of the church when they returned from their honeymoon. Chase kept changing her mind on what she wanted to serve and how to decorate. Page finally stopped the madness by suggesting they use a Hawaii theme since that was where the honeymoon was to be and to decorate and serve foods as if they were in Hawaii. That put Chase on a whole new tangent, but she was a great organizer. She personally contacted caterers to line everything up and took her friend, Jenny, to the party store to buy decorations. Page and Doug allowed her to take on the project fully, knowing that whatever she finally decided on would be wonderful.

The wedding was a quiet affair, attended by their closest friends and business associates. After all these years, they didn't want to make it too formal of an affair. When Page asked Ms. Yancy to give her away, Ms. Yancy replied, "You're darn tootin' I will give you away! I would expect no less!" Chase would be staying with her friend, Jenny, while they went on their honeymoon to Hawaii. Neither one had traveled there previously, so they were anxious to enjoy new sites and sounds. They had decided on an April wedding, giving them all a chance to limit their work and school schedules. Chase would be getting ready for graduation and had limited her spring extracurricular activities to study for finals. When Chase graduated, they would truly be a family, watching her receive her diploma. Page bought a white dress, but it was a short gown and had a small veil. Chase thought she looked very elegant, and they bought a blue dress that matched Chase's eyes in the same cut as the wedding dress. The wedding went off without a hitch, and Doug looked at Page as they left the church. "The past is gone, and we have nothing but blue skies from here on out." Page smiled, took Doug's hand, and kissed him soundly on the mouth. "Let's go, husband. I've waited years for this moment." They ran toward the car, showered by birdseed and bubbles and began the delayed life they had both wanted for so long. Blue skies indeed.

About the Author

Diane is from Southwest Nebraska and is an avid reader of all genre. She comes from a large family and grew up in a farming community. She was blessed with two children and now has four grandchildren. Her husband tries to help her with her story telling by suggesting silly ideas that have nothing to do with the current subject. Diane has dabbled in writing over several years and decided she wanted to have one of her stories to come alive. It was a long journey, but a happy one to complete. She can now check that off her bucket list.

Fic Win
Winters, Diane,
Blue skies

CPSIA information can be obtained
at www.ICGtesting.com
Printed in the USA
FFOW03n0337280517
36016FF